THE SHIP

was nearly ready, waiting to take Adam Reith
back to his home planet Earth . . .

The Foreverness was ready, and the
Pnume were waiting, to make Adam
Reith a crystallized, permanent dweller
of Tschai. He was an oddity, something
new, and the Pnume needed him for
their museum.

They also needed their books of Secrets,
though, and Adam Reith had that. All he
needed was someone who could read it in order to show him the exits from the Pnume
underground. But where, in all of Tschai, was
a single fugitive Earthman going to find an
ally against the most dreaded beings of that
planet?

The Pnume

JACK VANCE

DAW BOOKS, INC.
DONALD A. WOLLHEIM, PUBLISHER
New York

FIRST DAW PRINTING, AUGUST 1979

1 2 3 4 5 6 7 8 9

DAW■**ℑ**
BOOKS
DAW TRADEMARK REGISTERED
U.S. PAT. OFF. MARCA
REGISTRADA. HECHO EN U.S.A.

PRINTED IN U.S.A.

Chapter 1

In the warehouse at the edge of the Sivishe salt flats Aila Woudiver sat perched on a stool. A chain connected the iron collar around his neck to a high cable; he could walk from his table to the closet against the wall where he slept, the chain sliding behind him.

Aila Woudiver was a prisoner on his own premises, insult added to injury, which by all accounts should have provoked him to spasms of tooth-chattering fury. But he sat placidly on the stool, great buttocks sagging to either side like saddlebags, wearing an absurd smile of saintly forbearance.

Beside the spaceship which occupied the greater part of the warehouse Adam Reith stood watching. Woudiver's abnegation was more unsettling than rage. Reith hoped that whatever schemes Woudiver was hatching would not mature too quickly. The spaceship was nearly operative; in a week, more or less, Reith hoped to depart old Tschai.

Woudiver occupied himself with tat-work, now and then holding it up to admire the pattern—the very essence of patient affability. Traz, coming into the warehouse, scowled toward Woudiver and asserted the philosophy of the Emblem nomads, his forebears: "Kill him this moment; kill him and have an end!"

Reith gave an equivocal grunt. "He's chained by the neck; he does us no harm."

"He'll find a means. Have you forgotten his tricks?"

"I can't kill him in cold blood."

Traz gave a croak of disgust and stamped from the warehouse. Anacho the Dirdirman declared, "For once

I agree with the young steppe-runner: kill the great beast!"

Woudiver, divining the substance of the conversation, displayed his gentle smile. He had lost weight, so Reith noticed. The once-bloated cheeks hung in wattles; the great upper lip drooped like a beak over the pointed little chin.

"See him smirk!" hissed Anacho. "If he could he'd boil us in nerve-fire! Kill him now!"

Reith made another sound of moderation. "In a week we'll be gone. What can he do, chained and helpless?"

"He is Woudiver!"

"Even so, we can't slaughter him like an animal."

Anacho threw up his hands and followed Traz outside the warehouse. Reith went into the ship and for a few minutes watched the technicians. They worked at the exquisitely delicate job of balancing the power pumps. Reith could offer no assistance. Dirdir technology, like the Dirdir psyche, was beyond his comprehension. Both derived from intuitive certainties, or so he suspected; there was little evidence of purposeful rationality in any aspect of Dirdir existence.

Long shafts of brown light slanted through the high windows; the time was almost sunset. Woudiver thoughtfully put aside his fancy-work. He gave Reith a companionable nod and went off to his little room against the wall, the chain dragging behind him in a rattling half-catenary.

The technicians emerged from the ship as did Fio Haro the master mechanic. All went off to their supper. Reith touched the unlovely hull, pressing his hands against the steel, as if he could not credit its reality. A week—then space and return to Earth! The prospect seemed a dream; Earth had become the world remote and bizarre.

Reith went to the larder for a chunk of black sausage, which he took to the doorway. Carina 4269, low in the sky, bathed the salt flats in ale-colored light, projecting long shadows behind every tussock.

The two black figures which of late had appeared at sunset were nowhere to be seen.

The view held a certain mournful beauty. To the north the city of Sivishe was a crumble of old masonry tinted tawny by the slanting sunlight. West across Ajzan Sound stood the spires of the Dirdir city Hei and, looming above all, the Glass Box.

Reith went to join Traz and Anacho. They sat on a bench tossing pebbles into a puddle: Traz, blunt-featured, taciturn, solid of bone and muscle, Anacho, thin as an eel, six inches taller than Reith, pallid of skin, long and keen of feature, as loquacious as Traz was terse. Traz disapproved of Anacho's airs; Anacho considered Traz crass and undiscriminating. Occasionally, however, they agreed—as now, on the need to destroy Aila Woudiver. Reith, for his own part, felt more concern for the Dirdir. From their spires they could almost look through the portals of the warehouse at the work within. The Dirdir inactivity seemed as unnatural as Aila Woudiver's smile, and to Reith implied a dreadful stealth.

"Why don't they do something?" Reith complained, gnawing at the black sausage. "They must know we're here."

"Impossible to predict Dirdir conduct," Anacho replied. "They have lost interest in you. What are men to them but vermin? They prefer to chivy the Pnume from their burrows. You are no longer the subject of *tsau'gsh**: this is my supposition."

Reith was not wholly reassured. "What of the Phung or Pnume,** whatever they are, that come to watch us? They aren't there for their health." He referred to the two black shapes which had been appearing of late

---

tsau'gsh: prideful endeavor, unique enterprise, lunge toward glory. An essentially untranslatable concept.

** *Phung*: a man-like indigene of Tschai, given to erratic and reckless behavior.

Pnume: a diffident, tranquil and secretive folk, similar to the Phung but of lesser stature.

on the salt flats. Always they came to stand against the
sunset, gaunt figures wearing black cloaks and wide-
brimmed black hats.

"Phung go alone; they are not Phung," said Traz.
"Pnume never appear by daylight."

"And never so close to Hei, for fear of the Dirdir,"
Anacho said. "So, then—they are Pnumekin, or more
likely Gzhindra.*"

On the occasion of their first appearance the creatures stood gazing toward the warehouse until Carina
4269 fell behind the palisades; then they vanished into
the gloom. Their interest seemed more than casual;
Reith was disturbed by the surveillance but could
conceive of no remedy for it.

The next day was blurred by mist and drizzle; the
salt flats remained vacant. On the day following, the
sun shone once more, and at sundown the dark shapes
came to stare toward the shed, again afflicting Reith
with disquietude. Surveillance portended unpleasant
events: this on Tschai was an axiom of existence.

Carina 4269 hung low. "If they're coming," said
Anacho, "now is the time."

Reith searched the salt flats through his scanscope.**
"There's nothing out there but tussocks and swamp-
bush. Not even a lizard."

Traz pointed over his shoulder. "There they are."

"Hmmf," said Reith. "I just looked there!" He
raised the magnification of the scanscope until the
jump of his pulse caused the figures to jerk and
bounce. The faces, back-lit, could not be distinguished.
"They have hands," said Reith. "They are Pnumekin."

Anacho took the instrument. After a moment he

Pnumekin: men associated with the Pnume over a
period of tens of thousands of years, with consequent
assimilation of Pnume habits and mental processes.

Gzhindra: Pnumekin ejected from the underground
world, usually for reason of "boisterous behavior";
wanderers of the surface, agents for the Pnume.

**Scanscope*: photo-multiplying binoculars.

said: "They are Gzhindra: Pnumekin expelled from the tunnels. To trade with the Pnume you must deal through the Gzhindra; the Pnume will never dicker for themselves."

"Why should they come here? We want no dealings with the Pnume."

"But they want dealings with us, or so it seems."

"Perhaps they're waiting for Woudiver to appear," Traz suggested.

"At sunset and sunset alone?"

To Traz came a sudden thought. He moved away from the warehouse and somewhat past Woudiver's old office, an eccentric little shack of brick and flints, and looked back toward the warehouse. He walked a hundred yards further, out upon the salt flats, and again looked back. He gestured to Reith and Anacho, who went out to join him. "Observe the warehouse," said Traz. "You'll now see who deals with the Gzhindra."

From the black timber wall a glint of golden light jumped and flickered.

"Behind that light," said Traz, "is Aila Woudiver's room."

"The fat yellow shulk is signaling!" declared Anacho in a fervent whisper.

Reith drew a deep breath and controlled his fury: foolish to expect anything else from Woudiver, who lived with intrigue as a fish lives with water. In a measured voice he spoke to Anacho: "Can you read the signals?"

"Yes; ordinary stop-and-go code. '. . . Suitable . . . compensation . . . for . . . services . . . time . . . is . . . now . . . at . . . hand . . .' " The flickering light vanished. "That's all."

"He's seen us through the crack," Reith muttered.

"Or he has no more light," said Traz, for Carina 4269 had dropped behind the palisades. Looking across the salt flats, Reith found that the Gzhindra had gone as mysteriously as they had come.

"We had better go talk to Woudiver," said Reith.

"He'll tell anything but the truth," said Anacho.

"I expect as much," said Reith. "We may be informed by what he doesn't tell us."

They went into the shed. Woudiver, once again busy with his tat-work, showed the three his affable smile. "It must be close to suppertime."

"Not for you," said Reith.

"What?" exclaimed Woudiver. "No food? Come now; let us not carry our little joke too far."

"Why do you signal the Gzhindra?"

Beyond a lifting of the hairless eyebrows, Woudiver evinced neither surprise nor guilt. "A business affair. I occasionally deal with the under-folk."

"What sort of dealings?"

"This and that, one thing and another. Tonight I apologized for failing to meet certain commitments. Do you begrudge me my good reputation?"

"What commitments did you fail to meet?"

"Come now," chided Woudiver. "You must allow my few little secrets."

"I allow you nothing," said Reith. "I'm well aware that you plot mischief."

"Bah! What a canard! How should I plot anything trussed up by a chain? I assure you that I do not regard my present condition as dignified."

"If anything goes wrong," said Reith, "you'll be hoisted six feet off the ground by the same chain. You'll have no dignity whatever."

Woudiver made a gesture of waggish distaste and looked off across the room. "Excellent progress seems to have been made."

"No thanks to you."

"Ah! You minimize my aid! Who provided the hull, at great pains and small profit? Who arranged and organized, who supplied invaluable acumen?"

"The same man that took all our money and betrayed us into the Glass Box," said Reith. He went to sit across the room. Traz and Anacho joined him. The three watched Woudiver, now sulking in the absence of his supper.

"We should kill him," Traz said flatly. "He plans evil for all of us."

"I doubt that," said Reith, "but why should he deal with the Pnume? The Dirdir would seem the parties most concerned. They know I'm an Earthman; they may or may not be aware of the spaceship."

"If they know they don't care," said Anacho. "They have no interest in other folk. The Pnume: another matter. They would know everything, and they are most curious regarding the Dirdir. The Dirdir in turn discover the Pnume tunnels and flood them with gas."

Woudiver called out: "You have forgotten my supper."

"I've forgotten nothing," said Reith.

"Well, then, bring forth my food. Tonight I wish a white-root salad, a stew of lentils, gargan-flesh and slue, a plate of good black cheese, and my usual wine."

Traz gave a bark of scornful laughter. Reith inquired, "Why should we coddle your gut when you plot against us? Order your meals from the Gzhindra."

Woudiver's face sagged; he beat his hands upon his knees. "So now they torture poor Aila Woudiver, who was only constant to his faith! What a miserable destiny to live and suffer on this terrible planet!"

Reith turned away in disgust. By birth half-Dirdirman, Woudiver vigorously affirmed the Doctrine of Bifold Genesis, which traced the origin of Dirdir and Dirdirman to twin cells in a Primeval Egg on the planet Sibol. From such a viewpoint Reith must seem an irresponsible iconoclast, to be twarted at all costs.

On the other hand, Woudiver's crimes could not all be ascribed to doctrinal ardor. Recalling certain instances of lechery and self-indulgence, Reith's twinges of pity disappeared.

For five minutes longer Woudiver groaned and complained, and then became suddenly quiet. For a period he watched Reith and his companions. He spoke and Reith thought to detect a secret glee. "Your project approaches completion—thanks to Aila Woudiver, his craft, and his poor store of sequins, unfeelingly sequestered."

"I agree that the project approaches completion," said Reith.

"When do you propose to depart Tschai?"

"As soon as possible."

"Remarkable!" declared Woudiver with unctuous fervor. Reith thought that his eyes sparkled with amusement. "But then, you are a remarkable man." Woudiver's voice took on a sudden resonance, as if he could no longer restrain his inner mirth. "Still, on occasion it is better to be modest and ordinary! What do you think of that?"

"I don't know what you're talking about."

"True," said Woudiver. "That is correct."

"Since you feel disposed for conversation," said Reith, "why not tell me something obout the Gzhindra."

"What is there to tell? They are sad creatures, doomed to trudge the surface, though they stand in fear of the open. Have you ever wondered why Pnume, Pnumekin, Phung and Gzhindra all wear hats with broad brims?"

"I suppose that it is their habit of dress."

"True. But the deeper reason is: the brims hide the sky."

"What impels these particular Gzhindra out under the sky which oppresses them?"

"Like all men," said Woudiver, somewhat pompously, "they hope, they yearn."

"In what precise regard?"

"In any absolute or ultimate sense," said Woudiver, "I am of course ignorant; all men are mysteries. Even you perplex me, Adam Reith! You harry me with capricious cruelty: you pour my money into an insane scheme; you ignore every protest, every plea of moderation! Why? I ask myself, why? Why? If it were not all so preposterous, I could indeed believe you a man of another world."

"You still haven't told me what the Gzhindra want," said Reith.

With vast dignity Woudiver rose to his feet; the chain from the iron collar swung and jangled. "You had best take up this matter with the Gzhindra themselves."

He went to his table and after a final cryptic glance toward Reith took up his tatting.

Chapter 2

Reith twitched and trembled in a nightmare. He dreamt that he lay on his usual couch in Woudiver's old office. The room was pervaded by a curious yellow-green glow. Woudiver stood across the room chatting with a pair of motionless men in black capes and broad-brimmed black hats. Reith strained to move, but his muscles were limp. The yellow-green light waxed and waned; Woudiver was now frosted with an uncanny silver-blue incandescence. The typical nightmare of helplessness and futility, thought Reith. He made desperate efforts to awake but only started a clammy sweat.

Woudiver and the Gzhindra gazed down at him. Woudiver surprisingly wore his iron collar, but the chain had been broken or melted a foot from his neck. He seemed complacent and unconcerned: the Woudiver of old. The Gzhindra showed no expression other than intentness. Their features were long, narrow and very regular; their skin, pallid ivory, shone with the luster of silk. One carried a folded cloth: the other stood with hands behind his back.

Woudiver suddenly loomed enormous. He called out: "Adam Reith, Adam Reith: where is your home?"

Reith struggled against his impotence. A weird and desolate dream, one that he would long remember. "The planet Earth," he croaked. "The planet Earth."

Woudiver's face expanded and contracted. "Are other Earthmen on Tschai?"

"Yes."

14

The Gzhindra jerked forward; Woudiver called in a hornlike voice: "Where? Where are the Earthmen?"

"All men are Earthmen."

Woudiver stood back, mouth drooping in saturnine disgust. "You were born on the planet Earth."

"Yes."

Woudiver floated back in triumph. He gestured largely to the Gzhindra. "A rarity, a nonesuch!"

"We will take him." The Gzhindra unfolded the cloth, which Reith, to his helpless horror, saw to be a sack. Without ceremony the Gzhindra pulled it up over his legs, tucked him within until only his head protruded. Then, with astonishing ease, one of the Gzhindra threw the sack over his back, while the other tossed a pouch to Woudiver.

The dream began to fade; the yellow-green light became spotty and blurred. The door flew suddenly open, to reveal Traz. Woudiver jumped back in horror; Traz raised his catapult and fired into Woudiver's face. An astonishing gush of blood spewed forth—green blood, and wherever droplets fell they glistened yellow. . . . The dream went dim; Reith slept.

Reith awoke in a state of extreme discomfort. His legs were cramped; a vile arsenical reek pervaded his head. He sensed pressure and motion; groping, he felt coarse cloth. Dismal knowledge came upon him; the dream was real; he indeed rode in a sack. Ah, the resourceful Woudiver! Reith became weak with emotion. Woudiver had negotiated with the Gzhindra; he had arranged that Reith be drugged, probably through a seepage of narcotic gas. The Gzhindra were now carrying him off to unknown places, for unknown purposes.

For a period Reith sagged in the sack numb and sick. Woudiver, even while chained by the neck, had worked his mischief! Reith collected the final fragments of his dream He had seen Woudiver with his face split apart, pumping green blood. Woudiver had paid for his trick.

Reith found it hard to think. The sack swung and he felt a rhythmic thud; apparently the sack was being carried on a pole. By sheer luck he wore his clothes; the night previously he had flung himself down on his cot fully dressed. Was it possible that he still carried his knife? His pouch was gone; the pocket of his jacket seemed to be empty, and he dared not grope lest he signal the fact of his consciousness to the Gzhindra.

He pressed his face close to the sack hoping to see through the coarse weave, unsuccessfully. The time was yet night; he thought that they traveled uneven terrain.

An indeterminate time went by, with Reith as helpless as a baby in the womb. How many strange events the nights of old Tschai had known! And now another, with himself a participant. He felt ashamed and demeaned; he quivered with rage. If he could get his hands on his captors, what a vengeance he would take!

The Gzhindra halted, and for a moment stood perfectly quiet. Then the sack was lowered to the ground. Reith listened but heard no voices, no whispers, no footsteps. It seemed as if he were alone. He reached to his pocket, hoping to find a knife, a tool, an edge. He found nothing. He tested the fabric with his fingernails: the weave was coarse and harsh, and would not rip.

An intimation told him that the Gzhindra had returned. He lay quiet. The Gzhindra stood nearby, and he thought that he heard whispering.

The sack moved; it was lifted and carried. Reith began to sweat. Something was about to happen.

The sack swung. He dangled from a rope. He felt the sensation of descent: down, down, down, how far he could not estimate. He halted with a jerk, to swing slowly back and forth. From high above came the reverberation of a gong: a low melancholy sound.

Reith kicked and pushed. He became frantic, victim to a claustrophobic spasm. He panted and sweated and could hardly catch his breath; this was how it felt to go crazy. Sobbing and hissing, he took command of himself. He searched his jacket, to no avail: no metal, no cutting edge. He clenched his mind, forced himself to think. The gong was a signal; someone or something had been summoned. He groped around the sack, hoping to find a break. No success. He needed metal, sharpness, a blade, an edge! From head to toe he took stock. His belt! With vast difficulty he pulled it loose, and used the sharp pin on the buckle to score the fabric. He achieved a tear; thrusting and straining he ripped the material and finally thrust forth his head and shoulders. Never in his life had he known such exultation! If he died within the moment, at least he had defeated the sack!

Conceivably he might score other victories. He looked along a rude, rough cavern dimly illuminated by a few blue-white buttons of light. The floor almost brushed the bottom of the bag; Reith recalled the descent and final jerk with a qualm. He heaved himself out of the sack, to stand trembling with cramp and fatigue. Listening to dead underground silence, he thought to hear a far sound. Something, someone, was astir.

Above him the cavern rose in a chimney, the rope merging with the darkness. Somewhere up there must be an opening into the outer world—but how far? In the bag he had swung with a cycle of ten or twelve seconds, which by rough calculation gave a figure of considerably more than a hundred feet.

Reith looked down the cavern and listened. Someone would be coming in answer to the gong. He looked up the rope. At the top was the outer world. He took hold of the rope, started to climb. Up he went, into the dark, heaving and clinging: up, up, up. The sack and the cavern became part of a lost world; he was enveloped in darkness.

His hands burned; his shoulders grew warm and weak; then he reached the top of the rope. Groping, fumbling, he discovered that it passed through a slot in a metal plate, which rested upon a pair of heavy metal beams. The plate seemed a kind of trapdoor, which

clearly could not be opened while his weight hung on
the rope. . . . His strength was failing. He wrapped
the rope around his legs and reached out with an arm.
To one side he felt a metal shelf; it was the web of the
beam supporting the trapdoor, a foot or more wide. He
rested a moment—time was growing short—then
lurched out with his leg, and tried to heave himself
across. For a sickening instant he felt himself falling.
He strained desperately; with his heart thumping he
dragged himself across to the web of the beam. Here,
sick and miserable, he lay panting.

A minute passed, hardly long enough for the rope to
become still. Below four bobbing lights approached.
Reith balanced himself and heaved up at the metal
plate. It was solid and heavy; he might as well have
been shoving at the mountainside. Once again! He
thrust with all his might, without the slightest effect.
The lights were below, carried by four dark shapes.
Reith pressed back against the vertical section of the
beam.

The four below moved slowly in eerie silence, like
creatures underwater. They went to examine the sack
and found it empty. Reith could hear whispers and
mutters. They looked all around, the lights blinking
and flickering. By some kind of mutual impulse all
stared up. Reith pressed himself flat against the metal
and hid the pallid blotch of his face. The glow of the
lights played past him, upon the trapdoor, which he
saw to be locked by four twist-latches controlled from
above. The lights, veering away, searched the sides of
the shaft. The folk below stood in puzzled consultation.
After a final inspection of the cavern, a last flicker of
light up the shaft, they returned the way they had
come, flashing their lights from side to side.

Reith huddled high in the dark, wondering whether
he might not still be dreaming. But the sad desolate
circumstances were real enough. He was trapped. He
could not raise the door above him; it might not be
opened again for weeks. Unthinkable to crouch bat-
like, waiting. For better or worse, Reith made up his

mind. He looked down the passage; the lights, bobbing will-o'-the-wisps, were already far and dim. He slid down the rope and set off in pursuit, running with long gliding steps. He had a single notion, a desperate hope rather than a plan: to isolate one of the dark figures and somehow force him to lead the way to the surface. Above burned the first of the dim blue buttons, casting a glow dimmer than moonlight, but sufficient to show a way winding between rock buttresses advancing alternately from either side.

Reith presently caught up with the four, who moved slowly, investigating the passage to either side in a hesitant, perplexed fashion. Reith began to feel an insane exhilaration, as if he were already dead and invulnerable. He thought to pick up a pebble and toss it at the dark figures . . . Hysteria! The notion instantly sobered him. If he wanted to survive he must take a grip on himself.

The four moved with uneasy deliberation, whispering and muttering among themselves. Dodging from one pocket of shadow to another Reith approached as closely as he dared, to be ready in case one should detach himself. Except for a fleeting glimpse in the dungeons at Pera, he had never seen a Pnume. These, from what Reith could observe of their posture and gait, seemed human.

The passage opened into a cavern with almost purposeful roughness—or perhaps the rudeness concealed a delicacy beyond Reith's understanding, as in the case of a shoulder of quartz thrusting forth to display a coruscation of pyrite crystals.

The area seemed to be a junction, a node, a place of importance, with three other passages leading away. An area at the center had been floored with smooth stone slabs; light somewhat stronger than that in the cavern issued from luminous grains in the overhead rock.

A fifth individual stood to the side; like the others he wore a black cloak and a wide-brimmed black hat. Reith, flat as a cockroach, slid forward into a pocket of dense shadow close by the chamber. The fifth individual was also a Pnumekin; Reith could see his long visage, dismal, white and bleak. For an interval he took no notice of the first four and they appeared not to see him, a curious ritual of mutual disregard which aroused Reith's interest. Gradually the five seemed to wander together, none looking directly at the others.

There came a hushed murmur of voices. Reith strained to listen. They spoke the universal tongue of Tschai; so much he could understand from the intonations. The four reported the circumstances attendant upon finding the empty sack; the fifth, an official or monitor, made the smallest possible indication of dismay. It seemed that restraint, unobtrusiveness, delicacy of allusion were key aspects of sub-Tschai existence.

They wandered across the chamber and into the cavern close by Reith, who pressed himself against the wall. The group halted not ten feet distant, and Reith could now hear the conversation.

One spoke in a careful, even voice; ". . . Delivery. This is not known; nothing was found."

Another said: "The passage was empty. If defalcation occurred before the bag was lowered, here would be an explanation."

"Imprecision," said the monitor. "The bag would not then have been lowered."

"Imprecision exists in either case. The passage was clear and empty."

"He must still be there," said the tunnel monitor; "he cannot be anywhere else."

"Unless a secret adit enters the passage, of which he knows."

The monitor stood straight, arms at his sides. "The presence of such an adit is not known to me. The explanation is remotely conceivable. You must make a new and absolutely thorough search; I will inquire as to the possibility of such a secret adit."

The passage-tenders returned slowly along the cavern, lights flickering up and down, back and forth. The monitor stood looking after them. Reith tensed himself: a critical moment. Turning in one direction the monitor must certainly see Reith, not six feet away. If he turned in the other direction Reith was temporarily secure. . . . Reith considered an attack upon the man. But the four were still close at hand; a cry, a sound, a scuffle would attract their attention. Reith contained himself.

The monitor turned away from Reith. Walking softly he crossed the chamber and entered one of the side passages. Reith followed, running on the balls of his feet. He peered down the passage. Each wall was a ledge of pyroxilite. Remarkable crystals thrust forth from either side, some a foot in diameter, faceted like brilliants: russet-brown, black-brown, greenish-black. They had been artfully cleaned and polished, to show to best advantage: enormous effort had been spent in this corridor. The crystals offered convenient objects behind which to take concealment; Reith set off at a soundless lope after the gliding Pnumekin, hoping to take him unawares and put him in fear of his life: a primitive and desperate plan, but Reith could think of nothing better. . . . The Pnumekin halted, and Reith jumped nervously behind a shoulder of glossy olive crystals. The Pnumekin, after a glance up and down the passage, reached to the wall, pushed at a small crystal, touched another. A segment of the wall fell aside. The Pnumekin stepped through; the portal closed. The passage was empty. Reith was now angry with himself. Why had he paused? When the Pnumekin had halted Reith should have been upon him.

He looked up and down the corridor. No one in sight. He went on at a fast trot and after a hundred yards came abruptly upon the rim of a great shaft. Far below gleamed dim yellow lights and a motion of bulky objects which Reith could not identify.

Reith returned to the door through which the Pnumekin had disappeared. He paused, his mind racing with angry schemes. For a desperate wretch like himself any course of action was risky, but the sure way to disaster was inanition. Reith reached out and worked at the rock as he had seen the Pnumekin do. The door fell aside. Reith drew back, ready for anything. He looked into a chamber thirty feet in diameter: a conference room, or so Reith deduced from the round central table, the benches, the shelves and cabinets.

He stepped through the opening and the door closed behind him. He looked around the chamber. Light-grains powdered the ceiling; the walls had been meticulously chipped and ground to enhance the crystalline structure of the rock. To the right an arched corridor, plastered in white, led away; to the left were shelves, cabinets, a closet.

From the corridor came a dull staccato knocking, a sound which carried a message of urgency. Reith, already as taut as a burglar, looked around in a panic for a place to hide. He ran to the closet, slid the door ajar, pushed aside the black cloaks hanging from hooks, and squeezed within. The cloaks and the black hats at the back gave off a musty odor. Reith's stomach gave a jerk. He huddled back and slid the door shut. Putting his eye to a crack, he looked out into the room.

Time stood still. Reith's stomach began to jerk with tension. The Pnumekin monitor returned to the chamber, to stand as if in deep thought. The queer wide-brimmed hat shadowed his austere features, which, Reith noted, were almost classically regular. Reith thought of the other man-composites of Tschai, all more or less mutated toward their host-race: the Dirdirmen—sinister absurdities; the stupid and brutish Chaschmen; the venal over-civilized Wankhmen. The essential humanity of all these, except perhaps in the case of the Dirdirman Immaculates, remained intact. The Pnumekin, on the other hand, had undergone no perceptible physical evolvement, but their psyches had altered; they seemed as remote as specters.

The creature across the room—Reith could not think of him as a man—stood quiet without a twitch to his features, just inconveniently too distant for a lurch and a lunge out of the closet.

Reith began to feel cramped. He shifted his position,

producing a small sound. In a cold sweat he pressed his eye to the crack. The Pnumekin stood absorbed in reverie. Reith willed him to approach, urged him closer, closer, closer. . . . A thought came to disturb him: suppose the creature refused to heed a threat against his life? Perhaps it lacked the ability to feel fear. . . . The portal swung ajar; another Pnumekin entered: one of the passage-tenders. The two looked aside, ignoring each other. The newcomer spoke in a soft voice, as if musing aloud: "The delivery cannot be found. The passage and shaft have been scrutinized."

The tunnel monitor made no response. Silence, of an eery dream-like quality, ensued.

The passage-tender spoke again. "He could not have passed us. Delivery was not made, or else he escaped by an adit unknown to us. These are the alternate possibilities."

The monitor spoke. "The information is noted. Transit control should be instituted at Ziad Level, Zud-Dan-Ziad, at Ferstan Node Six, at Lul-lil Node and at Foreverness Station."

"Such will be the situation."

A Pnume came into the chamber, using an aperture beyond Reith's range of vision. The Pnumekin paid no heed, not so much as glancing aside. Reith studied the oddly jointed creature: the first Pnume he had seen, except for a darkling glimpse in the dungeons of Pera. It stood about the height of a man and within its voluminous black cloak seemed slight, even frail. A black hat shaded its eye-sockets; its visage, the cast and color of a horse's skull, was expressionless; under the lower edge a complicated set of rasping and chewing parts surrounded a near-invisible mouth. The articulation of the creature's legs worked in reverse to that of the human: it moved forward with the motion of a man walking backward. The narrow feet were bare and mottled, dark red and black; three arched toes tapped the ground as a nervous man might tap his fingers.

The Pnumekin tunnel monitor spoke softly into the

air. "An abnormal situation, when an item of delivery is no more than an empty sack. The passage and the shaft have been scrutinized; the item either was not delivered, or it made evasion by using a secret adit of Quality Seven or higher."

Silence. From the Pnume, in a husky muffled murmur, came words. "Verification of delivery cannot be made. The possibility of a classified adit exists, above Quality Ten, and beyond the scope of my secrets.* We may properly solicit information from the Section Warden."**

The tunnel monitor spoke in a voice of tentative inquiry. "The delivery, then, is an item of interest?"

The Pnume's toes drummed the floor with the delicacy of a pianist's fingers. "It is for Foreverness: a creature from contemporary Man-planet. Decision was made to take it."

Reith, cramped in the locker, wondered why the decision had been delayed so long. He eased his position, gritting his teeth against the possibility of a sound. When once again he put his eye to the crack the Pnume had departed. The monitor and the passage-tender stood quietly, taking no notice of each other.

Time passed, how long Reith could not judge. His muscles throbbed and ached, and now he feared to shift his position. He took a long slow breath and composed himself to patience.

At odd intervals the Pnumekin spoke in murmurs, looking aside all the while as if they addressed the air. Reith distinguished a phrase or two: ". . . The condition of Man-planet; there is no knowing . . ." ". . .

* *Secrets*: the rough translation of a phrase signifying the body of lore proper and suitable to a particular status. In the context of Pnume society the word *secrets* conveys more accurate overtones.
** Again, a rude rendering of an untranslatable idea: the title in Tschai terms connotes superlative erudition in combination with high authority and status.

Barbarians, surface dwellers, mad as Gzhindra . . ."
". . . Valuable item, invisible . . ."

The Pnume reappeared, followed by another: a creature tall and gaunt, stepping with the soft tread of a fox. It carried a rectangular case, which it placed with delicate precision upon a bench three feet in front of Reith; then it seemed to lose itself in reverie. A moment passed. The passage-tender of lowest status spoke first. "When a delivery is signaled by the gong, the bag is usually heavy. An empty bag is cause for perplexity. Delivery evidently was not made, or the item gained access to a secret adit, over Ten in Quality."

The Warden turned aside and, spreading wide its black cloak, touched the locks of the leather case. The two Pnumekin and the first Pnume interested themselves in the crystals of the wall.

Opening the case, the Warden brought forth a portfolio bound in limp blue leather. The Warden spread it apart with reverent care, turned pages, studied a tangle of colored lines. The Warden closed the portfolio, replaced it in the case. After a moment of musing, he spoke in a voice so breathy and soft that Reith had difficulty understanding him. "An ancient adit of Quality Fourteen exists. It courses nine hundred yards northward, descends, and enters the Jha Nu."

The Pnumekin were silent. The first Pnume spoke. "If the item came into the Jha Nu, he might traverse the balcony, descend by Oma-Five into the Upper Great Lateral. He could then turn aside into Blue Rise, or even Zhu Overlook, and so reach the *ghaun*."*

The Warden spoke. "All this only if the item has knowledge of the secrets. If we assume his use of a Quality Fourteen adit, then we can assume the rest. The manner by which our secrets have been disseminated—if this is the case—is not clear."

---

* *Ghaun*: a wild region exposed to wind and weather. In the special usage of the Pnume: the surface of Tschai, with emphasized connotations of exposure, oppressive emptiness, desolation.

"Perplexing," murmured the passage-tender.

The monitor said, "If a *ghian** knows Quality Fourteen secrets, how can these be safe from the Dirdir?"

The toes of both Pnume arched and tapped the stone floor.

"The circumstances are not yet clear," remarked the Warden. "A study of the adit will provide exact information."

The low-status passage-tenders were first to leave the room. The monitor, apparently lost in reflection, sidled after them, leaving the two Pnume standing still and rigid as a pair of insects. The first Pnume went off, padding on soft, forward-kicking strides. The Warden remained. Reith wondered if he should not burst forth and attempt to overpower the Warden. He restrained himself. If the Pnume shared the fantastic strength of the Phung, Reith would be at a terrible disadvantage. Another consideration: would the Pnume become pliant with pressure? Reith could not know. He suspected not.

The Warden took up the leather case and turned a deliberate stare to all quarters of the chamber. It appeared to listen. Moving with uncharacteristic abruptness, it carried the case to an expanse of blank wall. Reith watched in fascination. The Warden slid forward its foot, delicately touched three knobs of rock with its toes. A section of wall fell back, revealing a cavity into which the Warden tucked the case. The rock slid back; the wall was solid. The Warden went off after the others.

---

* *Ghian*: an inhabitant of the *ghaun*: a surface-dweller.

Chapter 3

The room was empty. Reith stumbled forth from the closet. He hobbled across the room. The wall showed no crack, no seam. The workmanship was of microscopic accuracy.

Reith bent low, touched the three protuberances. The rock moved back and aside. Reith brought forth the case. After the briefest of hesitations, he opened the case, removed the portfolio. From the closet he brought a carton of small dark bottles, approximately the same weight as the portfolio, which he closed into the case, and replaced all into the cavity. He touched the knobs; the cavity closed; the wall was solid rock.

Reith stood in the center of the room, holding the portfolio, obviously a valuable article. If he were able to evade detection and capture, if he were able to decipher the Pnume orthography—all of which seemed intrinsically unlikely—he might conceivably discover a route to the surface.

From the closet he brought a cloak, which he draped about himself, and a hat, somewhat too small, but which by dint of twisting and stretching he managed to pull low over his head. The Pnumekin habit of furtive unobtrusiveness would serve him well; no one would attempt greater furtiveness, less obtrusiveness, than himself. Now he must leave the immediate area, and find some secluded spot where he might examine the portfolio at his leisure. He tucked the portfolio into his jacket and set off along the white plastered corridor, putting one foot softly in front of the other as he had seen the Pnumekin do.

The corridor stretched long and empty ahead, at last opening upon a balcony which overlooked a long room, from which came a hum and shuffle of activity.

The floor of the chamber was twenty feet below. On the walls were charts and ideograms; in the center Pnumekin children took instruction. Reith had come upon a Pnumekin school.

Standing back in the shadows Reith was able to look down without fear of detection. He saw three groups of children, both male and female, twenty to each group. Like their elders they wore black cloaks and hats with flattened crowns. The small white faces were peaked and pinched, and almost laughably earnest. None spoke; staring into empty air they marched softly and solemnly through a drill or exercise. They were attended by three Pnumekin women of indefinite age, cloaked like the males and distinguishable only by lesser stature and somewhat less harshness of feature.

The children padded on and on through the exercise, the silence broken only by the shuffle of their feet. Nothing could be learned here, thought Reith. He looked in both directions, then set off to the left. An arched tunnel gave upon another balcony, which overlooked a chamber even larger than the first: a refectory. Tables and benches were ranked down the middle, but the chamber was vacant except for two Pnumekin, who sat widely separated, crouched lower over bowls of gruel. Reith became aware of his own hunger.

He heard a sound. Along the balcony came a pair of Pnumekin, one behind the other. Reith's heart began to thump so loudly he feared they would surely hear the sound as they approached. He pulled down his head, hunched his shoulders, moved forward in what he hoped to be the typical Pnumekin gait. The two passed by, eyes averted, thoughts on matters far removed.

With somewhat more assurance Reith continued along the passage, which almost immediately expanded to become a roughly circular node, the junction for three corridors. A staircase cut from the natural gray rock curved down to the level below.

The corridors were desolate and dim; Reith thought them unpromising. He hesitated, feeling tired and futile. The charts, he decided, were of no great help; he needed the assistance, willing or otherwise, of a Pnumekin. He was also very hungry. Gingerly he went to the staircase and, after ten seconds of indecision, descended, begruding every step which took him farther from the surface. He came out into a small anteroom beside the refectory. A portal nearby gave upon what appeared to be a kitchen. Reith looked in cautiously. A number of Pnumekin worked at counters, presumably preparing food for the children in the exercise room.

Reith backed regretfully away, and went off down a side passage. This was dim and quiet, with only a few light-grains in the high ceiling. After a hundred feet the passage jogged to the side and came to an abrupt end at the brink of a drop-off. From below the sound of running water: more than likely a disposal-place for waste and garbage, Reith reflected. He halted, wondering where to go and what to do, then returned to the anteroom. Here he discovered a small storage chamber in which were stacked bags, sacks and cartons. Food, thought Reith. He hesitated; the chamber must frequently be used by the cooks. From the exercise room came the children, walking in single file, eyes fixed drearily on the floor. Reith backed into the storage room: the children would discern his strangeness far more readily than adults. He crouched at the back of the room, behind a pile of stacked cartons: by no means the most secure of hiding places, but not altogether precarious. Even if someone entered the chamber he stood a good chance of evading attention. Reith relaxed somewhat. He brought forth the portfolio and folded back the limp blue leather cover. The pages were a beautiful soft vellum; the cartography was printed with most meticulous care in black, red, brown, green and pale blue. But the patterns and lines conveyed no information; the legend was set forth in undecipherable characters. Regretfully Reith folded the portfolio and tucked it into his jacket.

From a counter in front of the kitchen the children took bowls and carried them into the refectory.

Reith watched through a cranny between the cartons, more than ever aware of hunger and thirst. He investigated the contents of a sack, to find dried pilgrim-pod, a leathery wafer highly nutritious but not particularly appetizing. The cartons beside him contained tubes of a greasy black paste, rancid and sharp to the taste: apparently a condiment. Reith turned his attention to the serving counter. The last of the children had carried their bowls into the refectory. The serving area was vacant, but on the counter remained half a dozen bowls and flasks. Reith acted without conscious calculation. He emerged from the storage room, hunched his shoulders, went to the counter, took a bowl and a flask and retreated hurriedly to his hiding place. The bowl contained pilgrim-pod gruel cooked with raisin-like nubbins, slivers of pale meat, two stalks of a celery-like vegetable. The flask held a pint of faintly effervescent beer, with a pleasantly astringent bite. To the flask was clipped a packet of six round wafers, which Reith tasted but found unpalatable. He ate the gruel and drank the beer and congratulated himself on his decisiveness.

To the serving area came six older children: slender young people, detached and broodingly self-sufficient. Peering between the cartons, Reith decided that all were female. Five passed by the counter taking bowls and flasks. The last to come by, finding nothing to eat, stood in puzzlement. Reith watched with the guilty awareness that he had stolen and devoured her supper. The first five went into the refectory, leaving the one girl waiting uncertainly by the counter.

Five minutes passed; she spoke no word, standing with her eyes fixed on the floor. At last unseen hands set another bowl and flask down on the counter. The

Pnumekin girl took the food and went slowly into the refectory.

Reith became uneasy. He decided to return up the stairs, to select one of the passages and hope to meet some lone knowledgeable Pnumekin who could be overpowered and put in fear for his life. He rose to his feet, but now the children began to leave the refectory, and Reith stood back. One by one, on noiseless feet, they filed into the exercise room. Once more Reith looked forth and once more retreated as now the five older girls issued from the refectory. They were alike as mannequins from the factory: slender and straight, with skins as pale and thin as paper, arched coal-black eyebrows, and regular, if somewhat peaked, features. They wore the usual black cloaks and black hats, which accentuated the quaint and eerie non-earthliness of the earthly bodies. They might have been five versions of the same person, although Reith, even as the idea crossed his mind, knew that each made sure distinctions, too subtle for his knowing, between herself and the others; each felt her personal existence to be the central movement of the cosmos.

The serving area was empty. Reith stepped forth and on long quick strides crossed to the stairs. Only just in time: from the kitchen came one of the cooks, to go to the storage room. Had Reith delayed another moment he would have been discovered. Heart beating fast, he started up the stairs. . . . He stopped short and stood holding his breath. From above came a soft sound: the pad-pad-pad of footsteps. Reith froze in his tracks. The sounds became louder. Down the stairs came the mottled red and black feet of a Pnume, then the flutter of black cloth. Reith hurriedly retreated, to stand indecisively at the foot of the stairs. Where to go? He looked about frantically. In the storage room the cook ladled pilgrim-pod from a sack. The children occupied the exercise-chamber. Reith had a single choice. He hunched his shoulders and stalked softly into the refectory. At a middle table sat a Pnumekin girl, she whose supper he had commandeered. Reith took what he considered the most inconspicuous seat and sat sweating. His disguise was makeshift; a single direct glance would reveal his identity.

Silent minutes passed. The Pnumekin girl lingered over the packet of wafers which she seemed especially to enjoy. At last she rose to her feet and started to leave the chamber. Reith lowered his head: too sharply, too abruptly—a discordant movement. The girl turned a startled glance in his direction and even now habit was strong; she looked past him without directly focusing her eyes. But she saw, she knew. For an instant she remained frozen, her face loose and incredulous; then she uttered a soft cry of terror, and started to run from the room. Reith was instantly upon her, to stifle her with his hand and thrust her against the wall.

"Be quiet!" Reith muttered. "Don't make any noise! Do you understand?"

She stared at him in a kind of horrified daze. Reith gave her a shake. "Don't make a sound! Do you understand? Nod your head!"

She managed to jerk her head. Reith took away his hand. "Listen!" he whispered. "Listen carefully! I am a man of the surface. I was kidnapped and brought down here. I escaped, and now I want to return to the surface. Do you hear me?" She made no response. "Do you understand? *Answer!*" He gave the thin shoulders another shake.

"Yes."

"Do you know how to reach the surface?"

She shifted her gaze, to stare at the floor. Reith darted a glance toward the serving area; if one of the cooks should happen to look into the refectory, all was lost. And the Pnume who had descended the stairs, what of him? And the balcony! Reith had forgotten the balcony! With a sick thrill of fear he searched the high shadows. No one stood watching. But they could remain here no longer, not another minute. He grasped the girl by the arm. "Come along. Not a sound, remember! Or I'll have to hurt you!"

He pulled her along the wall to the entrance. The

serving area was empty. From the kitchen came a grinding sound and a clatter of metal. Of the Pnume there was no sign.

"Up the stairs," whispered Reith.

She made a sound of protest; Reith clapped his hand over her mouth and dragged her to the staircase. "Up! Do as I say and you won't be harmed!"

She spoke in a soft even voice: "Go away."

"I want to go away," Reith declared in a passionate mutter. "I don't know where to go!"

"I can't help you."

"You've got to help me. Up the stairs. Quick now!"

Suddenly she turned and ran up the stairs, so light on her feet that she seemed to float. Reith was taken by surprise. He sprang after her, but she outdistanced him and sped down one of the corridors. In desperation she fled; in equal desperation Reith pursued, and after fifty feet caught her. He thrust her against the wall, where she stood panting. Reith looked up and down the corridor: no one was in sight, to his vast relief. "Do you want to die?" he hissed in her ear.

"No!"

"Then do exactly what I tell you!" growled Reith. He hoped that the threat convinced her; and indeed her face sagged; her eyes became wide and dark. She tried to speak, and finally asked: "What do you want me to do?"

"First, lead the way to a quiet place, where no one comes."

With sagging shoulders she turned away, and proceeded along the corridor. Reith asked suspiciously, "Where are you taking me?"

"To the punishment place."

A moment later she turned into a side corridor which almost at once ended in a round chamber. The girl went to a pair of black flint cabochons; looking over her shoulder like a fairy-tale witch, she pushed the black bulbs. A portal opened upon black space; the girl stepped through with Reith close behind. She touched a switch; from a light-panel came a wan illumination.

They stood on a ledge at the edge of a brink. A crazy insect-leg derrick tilted over profound darkness; from the end hung a rope.

Reith looked at the girl; she looked silently back at him with a kind of half-frightened, half-sullen indifference. Holding to the derrick, Reith looked gingerly over the brink. A cold draft blew up into his face, and he turned away. The girl stood motionless. Reith suspected that the sudden convulsion of events had put her into a state of shock. The tight hat constricted his head; he pulled it off. The girl shrank back against the wall. "Why do you take off the hat?"

"It hurts my head," said Reith.

The girl flicked her glance past him and away into the darkness. She asked in a soft muffled voice, "What do you want me to do?"

"Take me to the surface, as fast as you can."

The girl made no answer. Reith wondered if she had heard him. He tried to look into her face; she turned away. Reith twitched off her hat. A strange eerie face looked at him, the bloodless mouth quivering in panic. She was older than her underdeveloped figure suggested, though Reith could not accurately have estimated her age. Her features were wan and dreary, so regular as to be nondescript; her hair, a short black mat, clung to her scalp like a cap of felt. Reith thought that she seemed anemic and neurasthenic, at once human and non-human, female and sexless.

"Why do you do that?" she asked in a hushed murmur.

"For no particular reason. Curiosity, perhaps."

"It is intimate," she muttered, and put her hands up to her thin cheeks. Reith shrugged, uninterested in her modesty. "I want you to take me to the surface."

"I can't."

"Why not?"

She made no answer.

"Aren't you afraid of me?" Reith asked gently.

"Not so much as the pit."

"The pit is yonder, and convenient."

She gave him a startled glance. "Would you throw me into the pit?"

Reith spoke in what he hoped to be a menacing voice. "I am a fugitive; I intend to reach the surface."

"I don't dare help you." Her voice was soft and matter-of-fact. "The *zuzhma kastchai* would punish me." She looked at the derrick. "The dark is terrible; we are afraid of the dark. Sometimes the rope is cut and the person is never heard again."

Reith stood baffled. The girl, reading a dire meaning into his silence, said in a meek voice: "Even if I wished to help you, how could I? I know only the way to the Blue Rise pop-out, where I would not be allowed, unless," she added as an afterthought, "I declared myself a Gzhindra. You of course would be taken."

Reith's scheme began to topple around his head. "Then take me to some other exit."

"I know of none. Those are secrets not taught at my level."

"Come over here, under the light," said Reith. "Look at this."

He brought forth the portfolio, opened it and set it before her. "Show me where we are now."

The girl looked. She made a choking sound and began to tremble. "What is this?"

"Something I took from a Pnume."

"These are the Master Charts! My life is done. I will be thrown into the pit!"

"Please don't complicate such a simple matter," said Reith. "Look at the charts, find a route to the surface, take me there. Then do as you like. No one will know the difference."

The girl stared with a wild, unreasoning gaze. Reith gave her thin shoulder a shake. "What's wrong with you?"

Her voice came in a toneless mutter. "I have seen secrets."

Reith was in no mood to commiserate with troubles so abstract and unreal. "Very well; you've seen the charts. The damage is done. Now look again and find a way to the surface!"

A strange expression came over the thin face. Reith wondered if she had gone mad for a fact. Of all the Pnumekin walking the corridors, what wry providence had directed him to an emotionally unstable girl? . . . She was looking at him, for the first time directly and searchingly. "You are a *ghian*."

"I live on the surface, certainly."

"What is it like? Is it terrible?"

"The surface of Tschai? It has its deficiencies."

"I now must be a Gzhindra."

"It's better than living down here in the dark."

The girl said in her dull voice, "I must go to the *ghaun*."

"The sooner the better," said Reith. "Look at this map again. Show me where we are."

"I can't look!" moaned the girl. "I dare not look!"

"Come now!" snapped Reith. "It's only paper."

"Only paper! It crawls with secrets, Class Twenty secrets. My mind is too small!"

Reith suspected incipient hysteria, although her voice had remained a soft monotone. "To become a Gzhindra you must reach the surface. To reach the surface we must find an exit, the more secret the better. Here we have secret charts. We are in luck."

She became quiet and even glanced from the corner of her eyes toward the portfolio. "How did you get this?"

"I took it from a Pnume." He pushed the portfolio toward her. "Can you read the symbols?"

"I am trained to read." Gingerly she leaned over the portfolio, to jerk instantly back in fear and revulsion.

Reith forced himself to patience. "You have never seen a map before?"

"I have a level of Four; I know Class Four secrets; I have seen Class Four maps. This is Class Twenty."

"But you can read this map."

"Yes." The word came with sour distaste. "But I dare not. Only a *ghian* would think to examine such a powerful document. . . ." Her voice trailed away to a murmur. "Let alone steal it. . . ."

"What will the Pnume do when they find it is gone?"

The girl looked off over the gulf. "Dark, dark, dark. I will fall forever through the dark."

Reith began to grow restive. The girl seemed able to concentrate only on those ideas rising from her own mind. He directed her attention to the map. "What do the colors signify?"

"The levels and stages."

"And these symbols?"

"Doors, portals, secret ways. Touch-places. Communication stations. Rises, pop-outs, observation posts."

"Show me where we are now."

Reluctantly she focused her eyes. "Not this sheet. Turn back . . . Back . . . Back . . . Here." She pointed, her finger a cautious two inches from the paper. "There. The black mark is the pit. The pink line is the ledge."

"Show me the nearest route to the surface."

"That would be—let me look."

Reith managed a distant and reflective smile: once diverted from her woes, which were real enough, Reith admitted, the girl became instantly intense, and even forgot the exposure of her face.

"Blue-Rise pop-out is here. To get there one would go by this lateral, then up this pale orange ramp. But it is a crowded area, with administrative wickets. You would be taken and I likewise, now that I have seen the secrets."

The question of responsibility and guilt flickered through Reith's mind, but he put it aside. Cataclysm had come to his life; like the plague it had infected her as well. Perhaps similar ideas circulated in her mind.

She darted a quick sidelong glance again. "How did you come in from the *ghaun?*"

"The Gzhindra let me down in a sack. I cut my way

out before the Pnumekin came. I hope they decide that
the Gzhindra lowered an empty sack."

"With one of the Great Charts missing? No person
of the Shelters would touch it. The *zuzhma kastchai**
will never rest until both you and I are dead."

"I become ever more anxious to escape," said Reith.

"I also," remarked the girl with ingenuous simplic-
ity. "I do not wish to fall."

Reith watched her a moment or two, wondering that
she appeared to bear him no rancor; it was as if he had
come to her as an elemental calamity—a storm, a
lightning-bolt, a flood—against which resentment, ar-
gument, entreaty would have been equally useless. Already, he thought, a subtle change had come over her
attitude; she bent to inspect the chart somewhat less
gingerly than before. She pointed to a pale brown Y.
"There's the Palisades exit, where trading is done with
the *ghian*. I have never been so far."

"Could we go up at this point?"

"Never. The *zuzhma kastchai* guard against the
Dirdir. There is continual vigilance."

Reith pointed to other pale brown Y's. "These are
other openings to the surface?"

"Yes. But if they believe you to be at large, they
will block off here and here and here"—she pointed—
"and all these openings are barred, and these in Ixa
section as well."

"Then we must go somewhere else: to other sec-
tors."

The girl's face twitched. "I know nothing of such
places."

"Look at the map."

She did his bidding, running her finger close above
the mesh of colored lines, but not yet daring to touch
the paper itself. "I see here a secret way, Quality
Eighteen. It runs from the passage out yonder to Paral-

---

* *zuzhma kastchai*: the contraction of a phrase: *the
ancient and secret world-folk derived from dark rock
and mother-soil.*

lel Twelve, and it shortens the way by a half. Then we might go along any of these adits to the freight docks."

Reith rose to his feet. He pulled the hat over his face. "Do I look like a Pnumekin?"

She gave him a brief unsympathetic inspection. "Your face is strange. Your skin is dark from the *ghaun* weather. Take some dust and wipe it on your face."

Reith did as he was bid; the girl watched with an expressionless gaze; Reith wondered what went on in her mind. She had declared herself an outcast, a Gzhindra, without overmuch agony of the spirit. Or did she contrive a subtle betrayal? "Betrayal" was perhaps unfair, Reith reflected. She had pledged him no faith, she owed him no loyalty—indeed, something considerably the reverse. So how could he control her after they set forth through the passages? Reith pondered and studied her, while she became increasingly agitated. "Why do you look at me like that?"

Reith held out the blue portfolio to her. "Carry this under your cloak, where it won't be seen."

The girl swayed back aghast. "No."

"You must."

"I don't dare. The *zuzhma kastchai*—"

"Conceal the charts under your cloak," said Reith in a measured voice. "I'm a desperate man, and I'll stop at nothing to return to the surface."

With limp fingers she took the portfolio. Turning her back, and glancing warily over her shoulder at Reith, she tucked the portfolio out of sight under her cloak. "Come then," she croaked. "If we are taken, it is how life must go. Never in my dreaming did I expect to be a Gzhindra."

She opened the portal and looked out into the round chamber. "The way is clear. Remember, walk softly, do not lean forward. We must pass through Fer Junction, and there will be persons at their affairs. The *zuzhma kastchai* wander everywhere; if we meet one of these, halt, step into the shadows or face the wall; this is the respectful way. Do not move quickly; do not jerk your arms."

She stepped out into the round room and set off along the passage. Reith followed five or six paces behind, trying to simulate the Pnumekin gait. He had forced the girl to carry the charts; even so, he was at her mercy. She could run screaming to the first Pnumekin they came upon, and hope for mercy from the Pnume. . . . The situation was unpredictable.

They walked half a mile, up a ramp, down another and into a main adit. At twenty-foot intervals the narrow doorways opened into the rock; beside each was a fluted pedestal with a flat polished upper surface, the function of which Reith could not calculate. The passage widened and they entered Fer Junction, a large hexagonal hall with a dozen polished marble pillars supporting the ceiling. In dim little booths around the periphery sat Pnumekin writing in ledgers, or occasionally holding vague and seemingly indecisive colloquies with other Pnumekin who had come to seek them out.

The girl wandered to the side and halted. Reith stopped as well.

She glanced at him, then looked thoughtfully toward a Pnumekin in the center of the room: a tall haggard man with an unusually alert posture. Reith stepped into the shadow of a pillar and watched the girl. Her face was blank as a plate but Reith knew her to be reviewing the circumstances which had overwhelmed her pale existence, and his life depended on the balance of her fears: the bottomless gulf against the windy brown skies of the surface.

Slowly she moved toward Reith and joined him in the shadow of the pillar. For the moment at least she had made her choice.

"The tall man yonder: he is a Listening Monitor.*
Notice how he observes all? Nothing escapes him."

---

* A somewhat unwieldy translation of the contraction *gol'eszitra,* from a phrase meaning "supervisory intellect with ears alert for raucous disturbance."

For a period Reith stood watching the Listening Monitor, becoming each minute more disinclined to cross the chamber. He muttered to the girl, "Do you know another route to the freight docks?"

She pondered the matter. Having committed herself to flight, her personality had become somewhat more focused, as if danger had drawn her up out of the dreaming inversion of her former existence.

"I think," she said dubiously, "that another route passes by way of the work halls; but it is a long way and other Listening Monitors are on hand."

"Hmmf." Reith turned to watch the Listening Monitor of Fer Junction.

"Notice," he said presently, "he turns to look this way and that. When his back is toward us, I'll move to the next pillar, and you come after me."

A moment later the Monitor swung around. Reith stepped out into the chamber, sauntered to the nearest of the marble pillars. The girl came slowly after him, still somewhat indecisively, or so it seemed to Reith.

Reith could not now peer around the pillar without the risk of attracting the Monitor's attention. "Tell me when he looks away," he muttered to the girl.

"Now."

Reith gained the next pillar and, using a file of slow-moving Pnumekin as a screen, continued on to the next. Now a single open area remained. The Monitor swung about abruptly, and Reith ducked back behind the pillar: a deadly game of peek-a-boo. From a passage to the side a Pnume entered the chamber, coming softly on forward-padding legs.

The girl hissed under her breath, "The Silent Critic . . . take care." She drifted away, head downcast, as if in an abstraction. The Pnume halted, not fifty feet from Reith, who turned his back. Only a few strides remained to the north of the passage. Reith's shoulder blades twitched. He could bear to stand by the pillar no longer. Feeling every eye in the chamber pressing upon him he crossed the open area. With each step he expected a cry of outrage, an alarm. The silence became oppressive; only by great effort could he control the urge to look over his shoulder. He reached the mouth of the passage and turned a cautious glance over his shoulder—to stare full into the eye sockets of the Pnume. With pounding heart Reith turned slowly and proceeded. The girl had gone ahead. He called to her in a soft voice, "Run ahead; find the Class Eighteen passage."

She turned back a startled glance. "The Silent Critic is close at hand. I may not run; if he saw he would think it boisterous conduct."

"Never mind the decorum," said Reith. "Find the opening as fast as possible."

She quickened her step, with Reith coming behind. After fifty yards he risked a glance to the rear. No one followed.

The corridor branched; the girl stopped short. "I think we go to the left, but I am not sure."

"Look at the chart."

With vast distaste, she turned her back and brought the portfolio from under her cloak. She could not bring herself to handle it and gave it to Reith as if it were hot. He turned the pages till she said, "Stop." While she studied the colored lines, Reith kept his gaze to the rear. Far back, where the passage met Fer Junction, a dark shape appeared in the opening. Reith, every nerve jerking, willed the girl to haste.

"To the left, then at Mark Two-one-two, a blue tile. Style Twenty-four—I must consult the legend. Here it is: four press-points. Three—one—four—two."

"Hurry," Reith said, through gritted teeth.

She turned a startled look back down the passage. *"Zuzhma kastchai!"*

Reith also looked back, trying to simulate the Pnumekin gait. The Pnume padded slowly forward, but with no particular sense of purpose, or so it seemed to Reith. He moved off along the passage and overtook the girl. As she walked she counted the number marks at the base of the wall: "Seventy-five . . . eighty . . . eighty-five . . ." Reith looked back. There were now two black shapes in the corridor; from somewhere a second Pnume had appeared. "One hundred ninety-five . . . two hundred . . . two hundred and five . . ."

The blue tile, filmed with an antique red-purple luster, was only a foot from the floor. The girl found press-points and touched them; the outline of a door appeared; the door slid open.

The girl began to shake. "It is Quality Eighteen. I should not enter."

"The Silent Critic is following us," said Reith.

She gasped and stepped into the passage. It was narrow and dim and haunted by a faintly rancid odor Reith had come to associate with the Pnume.

The door slid shut. The girl pushed up a shutter and put her eye to the lens of a peephole. "The Silent Critic is coming. It suspects boisterous conduct, and wants to issue a punishment . . . No! There are two! He has summoned a Warden!" She stood rigid, eye pressed to the peephole. Reith waited on tenterhooks. "What are they doing?"

"They look along the corridor. They wonder why we are not in view."

"Let's get moving," said Reith. "We can't stand here waiting."

"The Warden will know this passage. . . . If they come in . . ."

"Never mind that." Reith set out along the passage and the girl came behind him. A queer sight they made, thought Reith, loping through the dark in the flapping black cloaks and low-crowned hats. The girl quickly became tired and further diminished her speed by looking over her shoulder. She gave a croak of resignation and halted. "They have entered the passage."

Reith looked behind. The door stood ajar. In the gap the two Pnume were silhouetted. For an instant they stood rigid, like queer black dolls, then they jerked into motion. "They see us," said the girl, and stood with her head hanging. "It will be the pit. . . . Well, then, let us go to meet them in all meekness."

"Stand against the wall," said Reith. "Don't move. They must come to us. There are only two."

"You will be helpless."

Reith made no comment. He picked up a fist-size rock which had fallen from the ceiling and stood waiting.

"You can do nothing," moaned the girl. "Use meekness, placid conduct. . . ."

The Pnume came quickly by forward-kicking steps, the white undershot jaws twitching. Ten feet away they halted, to contemplate the two who stood against the wall. For a half-minute none of the group moved or made a sound. The Silent Critic slowly raised its thin arm, to point with two bony fingers. "Go back."

Reith made no move. The girl stood with eyes glazed and mouth sagging.

The Pnume spoke again, in husky fluting voice. "Go back."

The girl started to stumble off along the passage; Reith made no motion.

The Pnume watched him nonplussed. They exchanged a sibilant whisper, then the Silent Critic spoke again. "Go."

The Warden said in an almost inaudible murmur, "You are the item which escaped delivery."

The Silent Critic, padding forward, reached forth its arm. Reith hurled the rock with all his strength; it struck full in the creature's bone-white face. A crunch, and the creature tottered back to the wall, to stand jerking and raising one leg up and down in a most eccentric manner. The Warden, making a throaty gasping sound, bounded forward.

Reith jumped back, snatched off his cloak, and in an insane flourish threw it over the Pnume's head. For a moment the creature seemed not to notice and came forward, arms outspread; then it became to dance and stamp. Reith moved cautiously in and away, looking for an instant of advantage, and the two in their soundless gyrations performed a peculiar and grotesque ballet. While the Silent Critic watched indifferently Reith seized the Warden's arm; it felt like an iron pipe. The other arm swung about; two harsh finger-ends tore across Reith's face. Reith felt nothing. He heaved, swung the Warden into the wall. It rebounded and moved quickly upon Reith. Reith slapped tentatively at the long pale face; it felt cool and hard. The strength of the creature was inhuman; he must evade its grip, which put him in something of a quandary. If he struck the creature with his fists he would only break his hands.

Step by step the Warden padded forward, legs bending forward. Reith threw himself to the ground, kicked out at the creature's feet, to topple it off balance; it fell. Reith jumped up to evade the expected attack of the Silent Critic, but it remained leaning gravely against the wall, viewing the battle with the detachment of a bystander. Reith was puzzled and distracted by its attitude; as a result the Warden seized his ankle with the toes of one foot and with an amazing extension reached the other foot toward Reith's neck. Reith kicked the creature in the crotch; it was like kicking the crotch of a tree; Reith sprained his foot. The toes gripped his neck; Reith seized the leg, twisted, applied leverage. The Pnume was forced around on its face. Reith scrambled down upon its back. Seizing the head, he gave it a sudden terrible jerk backward. A bone or stiff membrane gave elastically then snapped. The Warden thrashed here and there in wild palpitations. By chance it gained its feet and with its head dangling backward bounded across the tunnel. It struck the Silent Critic, who slumped to the ground. Dead? Reith's eyes bulged. Dead.

Reith leaned against the wall, gasping for breath. Wherever the Pnume had touched him was a bruise. Blood flowed down his face; his elbow was wrenched; his foot was sprained . . . but two Pnume lay dead. A little distance away the girl crouched in a shock-induced trance. Reith stumbled forward, touched her shoulder. "I'm alive. You're alive."

"Your face bleeds!"

Reith wiped his face with the hem of his cloak. He went to look down at the corpses. Drawing back his lips, he searched the bodies, but found nothing to interest him.

"I suppose we'd better keep on going," said Reith.

The girl turned and set off down the tunnel. Reith followed. The Pnume corpses remained to lie in the dimness.

The girl's steps began to lag. "Are you tired?" asked Reith.

His solicitude puzzled her; she looked at him warily. "No."

"Well, I am. Let's rest for awhile." He lowered himself to the floor, groaning and complaining. After a moment's hesitation she settled herself primly across the passage. Reith studied her with perplexity. She had put the struggle with the Pnume completely out of her mind, or so it seemed. Her shadowed face was composed. Astonishing, thought Reith. Her life had come apart; her future must seem a succession of terrifying question marks; yet here she sat, her face blank as that of a marionette, with no apparent distress.

She spoke softly: "Why do you look at me like that?"

"I was thinking," he said, "that, considering the circumstances, you appear remarkably unconcerned."

She made no immediate reply. There was a heavy silence in the dim passage. Then she said, "I float upon the current of life; how should I question where it carries me? It would be impudent to think of preferences; existence, after all, is a privilege given a very few."

Reith leaned back against the wall. "A very few? How so?"

The girl became uneasy; her white fingers twisted. "How it goes on the *ghaun* I don't know; perhaps you do things differently. In the Shelters* the mother-

---

* Shelters: an inexact rendering of a word combining concepts of ageless order, quiet and security, the complexity of a maze.

women spawn twelve times and no more than half—
sometimes less—survive . . ." She continued in a voice
of didactic reflection: "I have heard that all the women
of the *ghaun* are mother-women. Is this true? I can't
believe it. If each spawned twelve times, and even if six
went to the pit, the *ghaun* would boil with living flesh.
It seems unreasonable." She added, as a possibly dis-
connected afterthought, "I am glad that I will never
be a mother-woman."

Again Reith was puzzled. "How can you be sure?
You're young yet."

The girl's face twitched with what might have been
embarrassment. "Can't you see? Do I look to be a
mother-woman?"

"I don't know what your mother-woman look like."

"They bulge at the chest and hips. Aren't *ghian*
mothers the same? Some say the Pnume decide who
will be mother-women, and take them to the crêche.
There they lie in the dark and spawn."

"Alone?"

"They and the other mothers."

"What of the fathers?"

"No need for fathers. In the Shelters all is secure;
protection is not needed."

Reith began to entertain an odd suspicion. "On the
surface," he said, "affairs go somewhat differently."

She leaned forward, and her face displayed as much
animation as Reith had yet noticed. "I have always
wondered about life on the *ghaun*. Who chooses the
mother-women? Where do they spawn?"

Reith evaded the question. "It's a complicated situation. In due course I suppose you'll learn something
about it, if you live long enough. Meanwhile, I am
Adam Reith. What is your name?"

" 'Name'?* I am a female."

"Yes, but what is your personal name?"

The girl considered. "On the invoices persons are

---

* "Identification," "name," and "type" in the language
of Tschai are the same word.

listed by group, area and zone. My group is Zith, of Athan Area, in the Pagaz Zone; my ranking is 210."

"Zith Athan Pagaz, 210. Zap 210. It's not much of name. Still, it suits you."

At Reith's jocularity the girl looked blank. "Tell me how the Gzhindra live."

"I saw them standing out on the wastelands. They pumped narcotic gas into the room where I slept. I woke up in a sack. They lowered me into a shaft. That's all I know of the Gzhindra. There must be better ways to live."

Zap 210, as Reith now thought of her, evinced disapproval. "They are persons, after all, and not wild things."

Reith had no comment to make. Her innocence was so vast that any information whatever could only cause her shock and confusion. "You'll find many kinds of people on the surface."

"It is very strange," the girl said in a vague soft voice. "Suddenly all is changed." She sat looking off into the darkness. "The others will wonder where I have gone. Someone will do my work."

"What was your work?"

"I instructed children in decorum."

"What of your spare time?"

"I grew crystals in the new East Fourth Range."

"Do you talk with your friends?"

"Sometimes, in the dormitory."

"Do you have friends among the men?"

Under the shadow of the hat the black eyebrows rose in displeasure. "It's boisterous to talk to men."

"Sitting here with me is boisterous?"

She said nothing. The idea probably had not yet occurred to her, thought Reith; now she considered herself a fallen woman. "On the surface," he said, "life goes differently, and sometimes becomes very boisterous indeed. Assuming that we survive to reach the surface."

He brought out the blue portfolio. As if by reflex Zap 210 drew herself back. Reith paid no heed. Squinting through the dim light he studied the tangle of colored lines. He put his finger down, somewhat tentatively. "Here, it seems to me, is where we are now." No response from Zap 210. Reith, aching, nervous and exhausted, started to reprimand her for disinterest, then caught his tongue. She was not here for her own volition, he reminded himself; she deserved neither reprimands nor resentment; by his actions he had made himself responsible for her. Reith gave a grunt of annoyance. He drew a deep breath and said in his most polite voice, "If I recall correctly, this passage leads over here"—he pointed—"and comes out into this pink avenue. Am I right?"

Zap 210 looked down askance. "Yes. This is a most secret way. Notice, it connects Athan with Saltra; otherwise, one must go far around, by way of Fei'erj Node." Grudgingly she came closer and brought her finger to within two inches of the vellum. "This gray mark is where we want to go: to the freight-dock, at the end of the supply arterial. By Fei'erj it would be impossible, since the route leads through the dormitories and the metal-spinning areas."

Reith looked wistfully at the little red circles which marked the pop-outs. "They seem so close, so easy."

"They will certainly be guarded."

"What is this long black line?"

"That is the freight canal, and is the best route away from Pagaz Zone."

"And this bright green spot?"

She peered and drew a quick breath. "It is the way to Foreverness: a Class Twenty secret!" She sat back and huddled her chin into her knees. Reith returned to the charts. He felt her gaze and looked up to find her studying him intently. She licked her colorless mouth. "Why are you such an important item?"

"I don't know why I'm an 'item' at all." Though this was not precisely true.

"They want you for Foreverness. Are you of some strange race?"

"In a way," said Reith. He heaved himself painfully

to his feet. "Are you ready? We might as well be going."

She rose without comment and they set off along the
dim passage. They walked a mile and came to a white
wall with a black iron door at the center. Zap 210 put
her eye to the peep-lens. "A dray is passing . . . persons are near." She looked back at Reith. "Hold your
head down," she said in a critical voice. "Pull the hat
lower. Walk quietly, with your feet pointed straight."
She turned back to the peephole. Her hand went to the
door-catch. She pressed, and the door opened. "Quick,
before we are seen."

Blinking and furtive, they entered a wide arched
passage. The pegmatite walls were studded with enormous tourmalines which, excited to fluorescence by
some means unknown, glowed pink and blue.

Zap 210 set off along the passage; Reith followed at
a discreet distance. Fifty yards ahead a low dray
loaded with sacks rolled on heavy black wheels. From
somewhere behind them came the sound of hammers
tapping at metal and a scraping noise, the source of
which Reith never learned.

For ten minutes they plodded along the corridor. On
four occasions Pnumekin passed, shadowed faces averted, thoughts exploring areas beyond Reith's imagination.

The polished pegmatite altered abruptly to black
hornblende, polished back from veins of white quartz
which seemed to grow like veins over the black matrix,
the end-product of unknown centuries of toil. Far
ahead, the passage dwindled to a minute black half-
oval, which by insensible degrees grew larger. Beyond
was black vacancy.

The aperture expanded and surrounded them; they
came out on a ledge overlooking a void as black and
empty as space. Fifty yards to the right a barge,
moored against the dock, seemed to float in midair;
Reith perceived the black void to be the surface of a
subterranean lake.

A half dozen Pnumekin worked listlessly upon the dock, loading the barge with bales.

Zap 210 sidled into a pocket of shadow. Reith joined her, standing somewhat too close for her liking; she moved a few fastidious inches away. "What now?" asked Reith.

"Follow me aboard the barge. Say no word to anyone."

"No one objects? They won't put us off?"

The girl gave him a blank look. "Persons ride the barges. This is how they see the far tunnels."

"Ah," said Reith, "wanderlust among the Pnumekin; they go to look at a tunnel."

The girl gave him another blank look.

Reith asked, "Have you ever traveled on a barge before?"

"No."

"How do you know where this barge goes?"

"It goes north, to the Areas; it can go nowhere else." She peered through the gloom. "Follow me, and walk with decorum."

She set off along the dock, eyes downcast, moving as if in a reverie. Reith waited a moment, then went after her.

She paused beside the barge, looked vacantly across the black void; then, as if absentmindedly, she stepped across to the barge. She walked to the outboard side and merged with the shadow of the bales.

Reith imitated her demeanor. The Pnumekin on the dock, immersed in their private thoughts, paid him no heed. Reith stepped aboard the barge and then could not control the acceleration of his pace as he slipped into the shade of the cargo.

Zap 210, tense as wire, peered at the dock-workers. Gradually she relaxed. "They are disconsolate; otherwise they would have noticed. Do the *ghian* always lurch and lope when they move about?"

"I wouldn't be surprised," said Reith. "But no harm done. Next time—" He stopped short. At the far end of the dock stood a dark shape. It stirred, came slowly toward the barge, and entered the zone of illumination. "Pnume," whispered Reith. Zap 210 stood soundless.

The creature padded forward, oblivious to the dock-workers, who never so much as glanced aside. It stepped softly along the dock, and halted near the barge.

"It saw us," whispered the girl.

Reith stood heavy-hearted, bruises aching, legs and arms nerveless and dull. He could not survive another fight. In a husky whisper he asked, "Can you swim?"

A horrified gasp and a glance across the black void. "No!"

Reith searched for a weapon: a club, a hook, a rope; he found nothing.

The Pnume passed beyond the range of vision. A moment later they felt the barge tremble under its weight.

"Take off your cloak," said Reith. He slipped out of his own and, wrapping up the portfolio, shoved both into a crevice of the cargo. Zap 210 stood motionless.

"Take off your cloak!"

She began to whimper. Reith clapped his hand over her mouth. "Quiet!" He pulled the neck laces and, touching her fragile chin, found it trembling. He jerked off her cloak, put it with his own. She stood half-crouching in a knee-length shift. Reith, for all the urgency of the moment, resisted an insane desire to laugh at the thin adolescent figure under the black hat. "Listen," he said hoarsely. "I can tell you only once. I am going over the side. You must follow immediately. Put your hands on my shoulders. Hold your head from the water. Above all, do not splash or flounder. You will be safe."

Not waiting for her acknowledgment, he lowered himself over the side of the barge. The frigid water rose up his body like a ring of icy fire. Zap 210 hesitated only for an instant, then went over the side, probably only because she feared the Pnume more than the wet void. She gasped when her legs hit the water.

"Quiet!" hissed Reith. Her hands went to his shoulders; she lowered herself into the water, and in a panic threw her arms around his neck. "Easy!" whispered Reith. "Keep your face down." He drifted in under the gunwale, and gripped a bracket. Unless someone or something peered over the side of the barge, they were virtually invisible.

A half-minute passed. Reith's legs began to grow numb. Zap 210 clung to his back, chin at his ear; he could hear her teeth chattering. Her thin body pressed against him, trapping warm pockets of water which pulsed away when one or the other moved. Once, as a boy, Reith had rescued a drowning cat; like Zap 210 it had clung to him with desperate urgency arousing in Reith a peculiarly intense pang of protectiveness. The bodies, both frightened and wet, projected the same elemental craving for life. . . . Silence, darkness, cold. The two in the water listened. . . . Along the deck of the barge came a quiet sound: the click of horny toes. It stopped, cautiously started, then stopped once more, directly overhead. Looking up, Reith saw toes gripping the edge of the gunwale. He took one of Zap 210's hands, guided it to the bracket, then the other. Once free, he turned to face outward from the barge.

Unctuous ripples moved away from him; lenses of quince colored light formed and vanished.

The toes over Reith's head clicked on the gunwale. They shifted their position. Reith, lips drawn away from his teeth in a ghastly grimace, lunged up with his right arm. He caught a thin hard ankle, pulled. The Pnume croaked in dismal consternation. It teetered forward and for a moment leaned at an incredible angle, almost horizontal, supported only by the grip of its toes. Then it fell into the water.

Zap 210 clutched at Reith. "Don't let it touch you; it will pull you apart."

"Can it swim?"

"No," she said through chattering teeth. "It is heavy; it will sink."

Reith said, "Climb up on my back, take hold of the gunwale, pull yourself aboard the barge."

Gingerly she swung behind him. Her feet pushed against his back; she stood on his shoulder, then clambered aboard the barge. Reith laboriously heaved himself up after her to lie on the deck, totally spent.

Presently he gained his feet, to peer toward the dock. The Pnumekin worked as before.

Reith moved back into the shadows. Zap 210 had not moved. The shift clung to her underdeveloped body. She was not ungraceful, reflected Reith.

She noticed his attention and huddled back against the cargo.

"Take off your undergown and put on your cloak," Reith suggested. "You'll be warmer."

She stared at him miserably. Reith pulled off his own sodden garments. In horror almost as intense as she had shown toward the Pnume, she jerked herself around. Reith found the energy for a sour grin. With her back turned she draped the cloak over her shoulders and by some means unknown divested herself of her undergarments.

The barge vibrated, lurched. Reith looked past the cargo to see the dock receding. It became an oasis of light in the heavy blackness. Far ahead showed a wan blue glimmer toward which the barge silently moved.

They were underway. Behind lay Pagaz Zone and the way to Foreverness. Ahead was darkness and the Northern Areas.

Chapter 4

The barge carried a crew of two, who kept to the apron at the bow of the barge. Here was a small pantry, a cook-bench, an island of dim yellow illumination. There seemed to be at least two other passengers aboard, perhaps as many as three or four, who were even less obtrusive than the crew, and manifested themselves only at the pantry and the cook-bench. The food seemed to be free to the use of all. Zap 210 would not allow Reith to go forward for food. When the pantry and cook-bench were not in use Zap 210 procured food for both: cakes of pilgrim-pod meal, candied plum-shaped objects which might have been fruit or possibly leech-like insects, bars of meat-paste, sweet and salty wafers of a delicate crisp white substance which Zap 210 considered a delicacy, but which left an unpleasant aftertaste in Reith's mouth.

Time passed: how long Reith had no way of knowing. The lake became a river which in turn became an underground canal fifty or sixty feet wide. The barge moved without a sound, propelled, so Reith guessed, by electric fields cycling along the keel. Ahead gleamed a dim blue light serving as a fix for the barge's steering sensor; when one blue light passed overhead, another always shone far ahead. At long intervals the barge passed lonesome little piers and docks, with passages leading away into unknown fastnesses.

Reith ate and slept; how many times he lost count. His cosmos was the barge, the dark, the unseen water, the presence of Zap 210. With nothing but time and boredom, Reith set himself to the task of exploring her personality. Zap 210, on her part, treated Reith with suspicion, as if begrudging even the intimacy of conversation: a skittishness and prim reserve peculiar in a person who, to the best of his knowledge, had not even a distorted understanding of ordinary sexual processes. Primordial instinct at work, Reith surmised. But how in good conscience could he turn her loose on the surface in such a condition of innocence? On the other hand the prospect of explaining human biology to Zap 210 was not a comfortable one.

Zap 210 herself never seemed to become bored with the passage of time; she slept or sat looking off into the darkness as if she watched passing vistas of green fascination. Vexed with her self-sufficiency, Reith would occasionally join her, taking no notice of her slight shift of fastidious withdrawal. Conversation with Zap 210 was never exhilarating. She had unalterable preconceptions regarding the surface: she feared the sky, the wind, the space of the horizons, the pale brown sunlight. Her anticipations were melancholy: she foresaw death under the club of a yelling barbarian. Reith tried to modify her views but encountered distrust.

"Do you think that we are ignorant of the surface?" she asked in calm scorn. "The *zuzhma kastchai* know more than anyone; they know everything. Knowledge is their existence. They are the brain-life of Tschai; Tschai is body and bones to the *zuzhma kastchai*."

"And the Pnumekin: how do they fit into the picture?"

"The 'persons'? Long ago the *zuzhma kastchai* gave refuge to certain men from the surface, with some females and some mother-women. The 'persons' proved their diligence by polishing stones and perfecting crystals. The *zuzhma kastchai* provided peace, and so it has been, for all the ages."

"And where did men come from originally, do you know this?"

Zap 210 was uninterested. "From the *ghian,* where else?"

"Do they teach you of the sun and the stars and the other worlds of space?"

"They teach what we most want to learn, which is decorum and good conduct." She heaved a small sigh. "That is all behind me and gone; how the others would marvel at me now!"

So far as Reith could comprehend, Zap 210's principal emotion appeared to be for her own indecorous conduct.

The barge moved on. Blue glimmer appeared ahead, waxed to become a glare and pass overhead, with a new blue glimmer far in the distance. Reith became stale and restless. Darkness was almost complete, relieved only by a vague glow from the bow apron forward. The feminine voice of Zap 210, herself only a blur, began to work upon his imagination; certain of her mannerisms took on the semblance of erotic provocations. Only by conscious rational effort could he maintain his impersonality. How, he would ask himself, could she provoke or tease when she was totally unaware of the male-female relationship? Any urgings from her subconscious must seem a peculiar perversion, the most exaggerated form of "boisterous conduct." He remembered the vitality of her body when she had clung to him in the water; he thought of the look of her soaked body; he began to wonder if his instincts might not be more accurate than his reason. Zap 210, if she felt anything other than glumness and foreboding, gave no evidence, except a somewhat greater willingness to talk. For hours she spoke in a low monotone, of everything she knew. She had lived a remarkably drab life, thought Reith, without experience of gaiety, excitement, frivolity. He wondered as to the content of her imaginings, but of this she said nothing. She recognized differences in the personalities of her fellows: subtle variations of decorum and discretion which to her assumed the same significance as the more vehement personality traits of the surface. She was aware of biological differences between male and female, but apparently had never wondered as to their justification. All very strange, mused Reith. The Shelters would seem to be an incubator for a whole congeries of neuroses. Reith dared venture no inquiries; whenever the conversation skirted such matters, she became instantly taciturn. Had the Pnume bred sexdrive out of the Pnumekin? Did they administer depressants, drugs, hormones, to eliminate a troublesome tendency to over-reproduce? Reith asked a few cautious questions, to which Zap 210 gave such irrelevant and unapposite replies that Reith was sure she didn't know what he was talking about. From time to time, Zap 210 admitted, certain persons found the Shelters too staid; they were sent up to the surface, into the glare, the blowing winds, the empty nights with all the universe exposed, and never allowed to return below. "I wonder that I am not more fearful," she said. "Is it possible that I have always had Gzhindra tendencies? I have heard that so much space creates a distraction; I do not wish to be so affected."

"We're not on the surface yet," said Reith, to which Zap 210 gave a faint shrug, as if the matter were of no great importance.

Regarding the reproductive mechanisms of the Pnume she had no sure knowledge; she was uncertain whether or not the Pnume regarded the matter as secret, though she suspected as much. As to the relative number of Pnume and Pnumekin she was also uncertain. "There are probably more *zuzhma kastchai*. But many are never seen; they keep to the Deep Places, where the precious things are kept."

"What precious things?"

Again Zap 210 was vague. "The history of Tschai goes back beyond thought; just so far back go the records. The *zuzhma kastchai* are meticulous; they know everything that has ever happened. They consider Tschai to be a great conservatory, where every item, every tree, every rock is a cherished curio. Now there are off-world folk on the *ghian*: three different sorts, who have come to leave their artifacts."

"Three?"

"The Dirdir, the Chasch, the Wankh."

"What of men?"

" 'Men'?" Her voice took on a dubious tone. "I don't know. Perhaps men too are off-world. If so, four peoples sojourn in Tschai. But this has happened before; many times have strange folk come down to Old Tschai. The *zuzhma kastchai* neither welcome nor repel; they observe, they watch. They expand their collections; they fill the museums of Foreverness; they compile their archives."

Reith began to see the Pnume in a new light. It seemed that they regarded the surface of Tschai as a vast theater, on which wonderful millennium-long dramas were played out: the Old Chasch-Blue Chasch wars; the Dirdir invasion, followed by the Wankh counter-invasion; the various campaigns, battles, routs, and exterminations; the building of cities, the subsidence of ruins, the coming and going of peoples—all of which explained the acquiescence of the Pnume to the presence of alien races: from the Pnume point of view, they embellished the history of Tschai. As for Zap 210 herself, Reith asked if she had the same regard for Tschai. The girl make one of her small apathetic gestures: no, it meant nothing; she cared little one way or the other. Reith had a sudden insight into the processes of her psyche. Life for Zap 210 was a somewhat insipid experience to be tolerated. Fear was reserved for the unfamiliar; joy was beyond conjecture. He saw his own personality as it must appear to her: abrupt, brutal, crafty, harsh and unpredictable, in whom the worst excesses of boisterous conduct must always be feared. . . . A sad creature, thought Reith, inoffensive and colorless. Still, remembering the feel of her clinging to his neck, he wondered. Still waters ran deep. In the dark, with nothing to occupy his mind, imaginings came to stimulate him and arouse his fervor, whereupon Zap 210, somehow sensing his turmoil, moved uneasily off into the shadows, leaving Reith sourly amused by the situation. What could be going on in her mind?

Reith invented a new game. He tried to amuse her. He invented grotesque incidents, extravagant situations, but Zap 210 was the fairy-tale princess who could not laugh. Her single pleasure, insofar as Reith could detect, was the sweet-salt wafer which served as a relish to the otherwise bland food; unfortunately, the supply of these delicacies was quickly exhausted, a day or two after they had boarded the barge. Zap 210 was taken aback by the deficiency. "There is always *diko* in our diet—always! Someone has made a foolish mistake!"

Reith had never seen her quite so emphatic. She became morose, then listless, and refused to eat anything whatever. Then she became nervous and irritable, and Reith wondered if perhaps the *diko* contained a habit-forming drug to arouse so pronounced a craving.

For a period which might have been three or four days she spoke almost not at all, and kept as far from Reith as was practicable, as if she held Reith responsible for her deprivation, which was actually the case, reflected Reith. Had he not blundered rudely into her cool gray existence, she would be conducting her ordinary routine, nibbling *diko* whenever she was of a mind. Her sulkiness waned; she became almost talkative; she seemed to want reassurance, or attention, or—could it be?—affection. So it appeared to Reith, who found the situation as absurd as any he had known.

On and on through the dark moved the barge, from blue light to blue light to blue light. They passed along a chain of underground lakes, through still caverns draped with stalactites, then for a long period—perhaps three days—along a precisely straight bore, with the blue lights spaced ten miles apart. The bore gave into another set of caverns, where they once again saw a few lonesome docks: islands of dim yellow light. Then once again the barge rode a straight canal. The voyage was approaching its end—the feeling was in the air. The crew moved with a somewhat less deliberate gait, and the passengers on the starboard side went to stand on the forward apron. Zap 210, returning from the pantry with food, announced in a dolorous mutter: "We have almost come to Bazhan-Gahai."

"And where is this?"

"At the far side of the Area. We have come a long way." She added in a soft voice, "It has been a peaceful time."

Reith thought that she spoke with regret. "Is this place near the surface?"

"It is a trade center for goods from the Stang Islands and Hedaijha."

Reith was surprised. "We are far to the north."

"Yes. But the *zuzhma kastchai* may be waiting for us."

Reith looked anxiously ahead, at the far blue guide-light. "Why should they be?"

"I don't know. Perhaps they won't."

Blue lights, one after the other: Reith saw them pass with growing tension. He became tired, and slept; when he awoke, Zap 210 pointed ahead. "Bazhan-Gahai."

Reith rose to his feet. Ahead the gloom had lightened; the water showed a far luminous reflection. With dramatic majesty the tunnel widened; the barge moved forward, ponderous as fate. The cloaked shapes at the bow stood in silhouette against a great golden space. Reith felt a lifting of the spirit, a mysterious exaltation. The voyage which had started in cold and misery was at its end. The sides of the tunnel—fluted buttresses of raw rock—began to be visible, illuminated on one side, in black shadow on the other. The golden light was a blur; beyond, across calm water, white crags rose to a great height. Zap 210 came slowly forward, to stare into the light with a rapt expression. Reith had almost forgotten what she looked like. The thin face, the pallor, the fragile bones of jaw and forehead, the straight nose and pale mouth were as he recalled; additionally he saw an expression to which he could put no name: sadness, melancholy, haunted foreboding. She felt his gaze and looked at him. Reith wondered what she saw.

The passage opened and widened. A lake lay ahead, long and twisting. The barge proceeded along vistas of uncanny beauty. Small islands broke the black surface; great gnarled columns of white and gray rose to the vaulted ceiling far above. Half a mile ahead, under a beetling overhand, a dock became visible. From an unseen opening a shaft of golden light slanted into the cavern.

Reith could hardly speak for emotion. "Sunlight!" ne finally croaked.

The barge eased forward, toward the dock. Reith searched the cavern walls, trying to trace out a route to the gap. Zap 210 said in a soft voice, "You will attract attention."

Reith moved back against the bales, and again studied the side of the cavern. He pointed. "A trail leads up to the gap."

"Of course."

Reith traced the trail along the wall. It seemed to terminate at the dock, now only a quarter of a mile distant. Reith noticed several shapes in black cloaks: Pnume or Pnumekin, he could not be sure. They stood waiting in what he considered sinister attitudes; he became highly uneasy.

Going to the stern of the barge, Reith looked right and left. He returned to Zap 210. "In a minute or so we'll pass close to that little island. That's where we better leave the barge. I don't care to land at that dock."

Zap 210 gave a fatalistic shrug. They went to the stern of the barge. The island, a twisted knob of limestone, came abeam. Reith said, "Lower yourself into the water. Don't kick or flounder; I'll keep you afloat."

She gave him one unreadable side-glance and did as he bid. Holding the blue leather portfolio high in one hand he slid into the water beside her. The barge moved away, toward whomever or whatever waited on the dock. "Put your hands on my shoulders," said Reith. "Hold your face just above the water."

The ground rose under their feet; they clambered up on the island. The barge had almost reached the dock. The black shapes came forward. By their gait Reith knew them for Pnume.

From the island they waded to the shore, keeping to areas of shadow, where they were invisible to those on the dock, or so Reith hoped. A hundred feet above ran the trail to the gap. Reith made a careful reconnaissance, and they started to climb, scrambling over detritus, clinging to knobs of agate, crawling over humps and buttresses. A mournful hooting sound drifted across the water. Zap 210 became rigid.

"What does that mean?" Reith asked in a hushed voice.

"It must be a summons, or a call . . . like nothing I have heard in Pagaz."

They continued up the slope, sodden cloaks clinging to their bodies, and at last heaved themselves up on the trail. Reith looked ahead and back; no living creature could be seen. The gap into the outer world was only fifty yards distant. Once again the hooting sounded, conveying a mournful urgency.

Panting, stumbling, they ran up the trail. The gap opened before them; they saw the golden-gray sky of Tschai, where a tumbled group of black clouds floated. He took a last look down the trail. With the light of outdoors in his face, with tears blurring his vision, he could distinguish only shadows and dim rock-shapes. The underground was again a world remote and unknown. He took Zap 210's hand, pulled her out into the open. Slowly she stepped forward and looked across the surface. They stood halfway up the slope of a rocky hill overlooking a wide valley. In the distance spread a calm gray surface: the sea.

Reith took a final look over his shoulder at the gap, and started down the hill. Zap 210, with a dubious glance toward the sun, followed. Reith halted. He removed the hated black hat and sailed it off over the rocks. Then he took Zap 210's hat and did the same despite her startled protest.

Chapter 5

For Reith the walk down the wide valley in the brown-gold light of afternoon was euphoric. He felt light-headed; his torpor had vanished: he felt strong and agile and full of hope; he even felt a new and tolerant affection for Zap 210. An odd wry creature, he thought, watching her surreptitiously, and pale as a ghost. She clearly felt uneasy in this sudden wilderness of space. Her gaze moved from the sky, along the sweep of hills to either side, out to the horizon of what Reith had decided must be the First Sea.

They reached the floor of the valley. A sluggish stream wandered between banks of dark red reeds. Nearby grew pilgrim plant, the pods of which formed the indispensable staple food of Tschai. Zap 210 looked at the gray-green pods skeptically, failing to recognize the shriveled dry yellow tablets imported into the Shelters. She ate with fatalistic disinterest.

Reith saw her looking back the way they had come, somewhat wistfully, he thought. "Do you miss the Shelters?" he asked.

Zap 210 considered her reply. "I am afraid. We can be seen from all directions. Perhaps the *zuzhma kastchai* watch us from the gap. They may send night-hounds after us."

Reith looked up toward the gap: a shadow, almost invisible from where they sat. He could detect no evidence of scrutiny; they seemed alone in the open valley. But he could not be sure. Eyes could be watching from the gap; the black cloaks made them conspicuous. He looked toward Zap 210. Almost certainly she would refuse to remove the garment. . . . Reith rose to his feet. "It's growing late; perhaps we can find a village along the shore."

Two miles downstream the river spread wide to become a swamp. Along the opposite shore grew a dense forest of enormous dyans, the trunks on the periphery slanting somewhat outward. Reith had seen such a forest before; it was, so he suspected, a sacred grove of the Khors, a truculent folk living along the south shore of the First Sea.

The presence of the sacred grove, if such it was, gave Reith pause. An encounter with the Khors might immediately validate Zap 210's fears regarding the *ghaun,* and the unpleasant habits of those who lived there.

At the moment there were no Khors in sight. Proceeding along the verge of the swamp they came out on a knoll overlooking a hundred yards of mud flat, with the sluggish First Sea beyond. Far to right and left were crumbling gray headlands, almost lost in the afternoon murk. Somewhere to the southeast, perhaps not too far, must lie the Carabas, where men sought sequins and where the Dirdir came to hunt.

Reith looked up and down the coast, trying to locate himself by sheer instinct. Zap 210 stared glumly off to sea, wondering what the future held. A mile or so along the shore to the southeast Reith noticed the crazy stilts of a pier extending across the mud flats, out into the sea; at the end half a dozen boats were moored. A swelling of ground beyond the swamp concealed the village which must lie at the head of the pier.

The Khors, while not automatically hostile, lived by a complicated etiquette, transgressions of which were not tolerated. A stranger's ignorance received no sympathy; the rules were explicit. A visit with the Khors thus became a chancy occasion.

"I don't dare risk the Khors," said Reith. He turned to look back over the desolate hills. "Sivishe is a long way south. We'll have to make for Cape Braise. If we get there we can take passage by ship down the west coast, although at the moment I don't know what we'll use for money."

Zap 210 looked at him in slack-mouthed surprise. "You want me to come with you?"

So here was the explanation for her melancholy inspection of the landscape, thought Reith. He asked, "Did you have other plans?"

She pursed her lips sullenly. "I thought that you would want to go your way alone."

"And leave you by yourself? You might not fare too well."

She looked at him with sardonic speculation, wondering at the reason for his concern.

"There's a good deal of 'boisterous conduct' up here on the surface," said Reith. "I don't think you'd like it."

"Oh."

"We'll have to go warily. These cloaks—we'd better take them off."

Zap 210 looked at him aghast. "And go without clothing?"

"No, just without the cloaks. They attract attention and hostility. We don't want to be taken for Gzhindra."

"But that is what I must be!"

"At Sivishe you may decide otherwise. If we arrive, of course. We don't help ourselves going as Gzhindra." He pulled off his cloak. With her face angrily turned away she removed her cloak and stood in her gray undergown.

Reith rolled the cloaks into a bundle. "It may be cold at night; I'll take them with us."

He picked up the blue portfolio, which now represented excess baggage. He wavered a moment and at last slid the portfolio between the inner and outer layers of his jacket.

They set off to the northwest along the shore. Behind them the Khor grove became a dark blur; the far headland grew bulky and dark. Carina 4269 moved down the sky and the sunlight took on a late afternoon richness. To the north, however, a bank of purple-black clouds threatened one of the sudden Tschai thunderstorms. The clouds moved inexorably south, muffling, half-concealing spasms of electric light. The sea below shone with the sallow luster of graphite. Ahead, close underneath the headland, appeared another grove of dyan trees. A sacred grove? Reith searched the landscape but saw no Khor town.

The grove loomed above them, the exterior boles leaning outward, the fronds hanging down in a great parasol. The headland conceivably concealed a village, but at the moment, they were the only animate creatures under the half-black, half-golden-brown sky.

Reith imparted none of his misgivings to Zap 210, who was sufficiently occupied with her own. Exposure to the sunlight had flushed her face. In the rather flimsy and clinging gray undergown, with the black hair beginning to curl down on her forehead and her ears, she seemed a somewhat different person then the pallid wretch Reith had met in the Pagaz refectory. . . . Was his imagination at fault? Or had her body become fuller and rounder? She noticed his gaze and gave him a glare of shame and defiance. "Why do you stare at me?"

"No particular reason. Except that you look rather different now than when I first saw you. Different and better."

"I don't know what you mean," she snapped. "You're talking foolishness."

"I suppose so. . . . One of these days—not just now—I'll explain how life is on the surface. Customs and habits are more complicated—more intimate, even more 'boisterous'—than in the Shelters."

"Hmmf," sniffed Zap 210. "Why are you heading toward the forest? Isn't it another secret place?"

"I don't know." Reith pointed to the clouds. "See the black trails hanging below? That's rain. Under the trees we might stay dry. Then, night is coming soon,

and the night-hounds. We have no weapons. If we
climb a tree we'll be safe."

Zap 210 made no further comment; they approached the grove.

The dyans reared high overhead. At the first line of
boles they stopped to listen, but heard only a breath of
wind from the oncoming storm.

Step by step they entered the grove. The sunlight
shining past the clouds, projected a hundred shafts and
beams of dark golden light; Reith and Zap 210 walked
in and out of shadow. The nearest branches were a
hundred feet above; the trees could not be climbed; the
grove offered little more security from night-hounds
than did the open downs. . . . Zap 210 stopped short
and seemed to listen. Reith could hear nothing. "What
do you hear?"

"Nothing." But she still listened, and peered in all
directions. Reith became highly uneasy, wondering
what Zap 210 sensed that he did not.

They proceeded, wary as cats, keeping to the
shadows. A clearing free of boles opened before them,
shrouded by a continuous roof of foliage. They looked
forth into a circular area containing four huts, a low
central platform. The surrounding boles had been
carved to the semblance of men and women, a pair at
each tree. The men were represented with long nut-
cracker chins, narrow foreheads, bulging cheeks and
eyes; the females displayed long noses and lips parted
in wide grins. Neither resembled the typical Khor man
or woman, who, as Reith recollected, almost exactly
resembled one another in stature, physiognomy and
dress. The poses, conventionalized and rigid, depicted
the act of copulation. Reith looked askance at Zap
210, who seemed blankly puzzled. Reith decided that
she interpreted the not-too-explicit attitudes as
representations of sheer sportiveness, or simple "boisterous conduct."

The clouds submerged the sun. Gloom came to the
glade; drops of rain touched their faces. Reith scrutinized the huts. They were built after the usual Khor

style, of dull brown brick with conical black iron roofs.
There were four, facing each other at quadrants
around the clearing. They appeared to be empty. Reith
wondered what the huts contained. "Wait here," he
whispered to Zap 210, and ran crouching to the
nearest hut. He listened: no sound. He tried the door,
which swung back easily. The interior exhaled a heavy
odor, almost a stink, of poorly cured leather, resin,
musk. On a rack hung several dozen masks of sculp-
tured wood, identical to the male faces of the carved
trees. Two benches occupied the center of the room;
no weapons, no garments, no articles of value were to
be seen. Reith returned to Zap 210 to find her inspecting the carved treetrunks, eyebrows lifted in distaste.

A purple dazzle struck the sky, followed immediately by a clap of thunder; down came rain in a tor-
rent. Reith led the girl at a run to the hut. They
entered and stood with rain drumming upon the iron
roof. "The Khors are an unpredictable people," said
Reith, "but I can't imagine them visiting their grove on
a night like this."

"Why would they come at any time?" demanded
Zap 210 peevishly. "There is nothing here but those
grotesque dancers. Do the Khor look that that?"

Reith understood that she referred to the figures
carved upon the treetrunks. "Not at all," he said.
"They are a yellow-skinned folk, very neat and precise.
The men and women are exactly alike in appearance,
and disposition as well." He tried to recall what Anacho had told him: "A strange secret folk with secret
ways, different by day and by night, or at least this is
the report. Each individual owns two souls which come
and go with dawn and sunset; the body comprises two
different persons." Later, Anacho had warned: "The
Khor are sensitive as spice-snakes! Do not speak to
them; pay them no heed except from necessity, in
which case you must use the fewest possible words.
They consider garrulity a crime against nature. . . .
Never acknowledge the presence of a woman, do not
look toward their children: they will suspect you of

laying a curse. Above all ignore the sacred grove! Their weapon is the iron dart which they throw with accuracy. They are a dangerous people."

Reith paraphrased the remarks to the best of his recollection; Zap 210 went to sit on one of the benches.

"Lie down," said Reith. "Try to sleep."

"In the noise of the storm, and this vile smell to all sides? Are all the houses of the *ghaun* so?"

"Not all of them," muttered Reith. He went to look out the door. The alteration of lightning glare and dying twilight upon the tree-statues presented the illusion of a frantic erotic jerking. Zap 210 might soon begin to ask questions to which Reith did not dare to respond. . . . Upon the roof came a sudden clatter of hail; abruptly the storm passed over, and nothing could be heard but wind sighing in the dyan trees.

Reith returned into the room. He spoke in a voice which rang false even to his own ears: "Now you can rest; at least the sound is gone."

She made a soft sound which Reith could not interpret, and went herself to stand in the doorway. She looked back at Reith. "Someone is coming."

Reith hurried to the doorway and looked forth. Across the clearing stood a figure in Khor garments: male or female Reith could not determine. It went into the hut directly opposite their own. Reith said to Zap 210: "We'd better leave while we have a chance."

She held him back. "No, no! There's another one."

The second Khor, entering the clearing, looked up at the sky. The first came from the hut with a flaring cresset on a pole, and the second ran quickly to the hut in which Reith and Zap 210 were concealed. The first took no notice. As the Khor entered Reith struck hard, ignoring all precepts of gallantry; in this case male and female were all the same. The Khor fell and lay limp. Reith jumped forward; the Khor was male. Reith stripped off his cape, tied his hands and feet with sandal thongs and gagged him with the sleeve of his black coat. With Zap 210's help he dragged the man behind the rack of masks. Here Reith made a quick search of the limp body, finding a pair of iron darts, a dagger and a soft leather pouch containing sequins, which Reith somewhat guiltily appropriated.

Zap 210 stood by the door gazing out in fascination. The first to come had been a woman. Wearing a woman-mask and a white frock, she stood by the cresset which she had thrust into a socket near the central platform. If she were perplexed by the disappearance of the man who had entered the hut she gave no sign.

Reith looked forth. "Now: while there's only one woman—"

"No! More come."

Three persons slipped separately into the clearing, going to the other three huts. One, in a woman mask and white gown, emerged with another cresset which she placed in a socket and stood quietly like the first. The other two now came forth, wearing man-masks and white gowns like those of the women. They went to the central platform and stood near the woman, who made no movement.

Reith began to understand something of the purpose of the sacred grove. Zap 210 stared forth in fascination.

Reith became highly uneasy. If events proceeded as he suspected, she would be shocked and horrified.

Three more persons appeared. One came to the hut where Reith and Zap 210 waited; Reith tried to deal with him as he had the other; but this time the blow was glancing and the man fell with a startled grunt. Reith was instantly upon him and shut off his breath until he fainted. Using sandal thongs and cape as before he tied and gagged the Khor and again robbed the man of his pouch. "I regret becoming a thief," said Reith, "but my need is far greater than yours."

Zap 210, standing by the door, gave a startled gasp. Reith went to look. The women—now there were three—had disrobed to stand nude. They began to sing, a wordless chant, sweet, soft, insistent. The three in the man-masks began a slow gyration around the platform.

Zap 210 muttered under her breath: "What are they doing? Why do they reveal their bodies? Never have I seen such a thing!"

"It is only religion," said Reith nervously. "Don't watch. Go lie down. Sleep. You must be very tired."

She gave him a lambent look of wonder and distrust. "You don't answer my question. I am very embarrassed. I have never seen a naked person. Are all the folk of the *ghaun* so—so boisterous? It is shocking. And the singing: most disturbing. What are they planning to do?"

Reith tried to stand in front of her. "Hadn't you better sleep? The rites will only bore you."

"They don't bore me! I am astounded that people can be so bold! And look! The men!"

Reith took a deep breath and came to a desperate decision. "Come back here." He gave her a female mask. "Put that on."

She jerked back aghast. "What for?"

Reith took a man-mask and fitted it over his face. "We're leaving."

"But—" She turned a fascinated look toward the platform.

Reith pulled her back around, fitted one of the Khor hats on her head, arranged the other on his own.

"They'll certainly see us," said Zap 210. "They'll chase us and kill us."

"Perhaps so," said Reith. "Nevertheless we'd better go." He looked around the clearing. "You go first. Walk behind the hut. I'll come after you."

Zap 210 departed the hut. The woman at the platform chanted with the most compelling urgency; the men stood nude.

Reith joined Zap 210 behind the hut. Had they been noticed? The chanting continued, rising and falling. "Walk out into the grove. Don't look back."

"Ridiculous," muttered Zap 210. "Why shouldn't I look back?" She marched toward the forest, with Reith twenty feet behind her. From the hut came a wild scream of fury. The chanting stopped short. There was stunned silence.

"Run," said Reith. Through the sacred grove they fled, throwing away the hats and masks. From behind came calls of passionate fury, but deterred perhaps by their nudity, the Khor offered no pursuit.*

Reith and Zap 210 came to the edge of the grove. They paused to catch their breath. Halfway up the sky the blue moon shone through a few ragged clouds; elsewhere the sky was clear.

Zap 210 looked up. "What are those little lights?"

"Those are stars," said Reith. "Far suns. Most control a family of planets. From a world called Earth, men came: your ancestors, mine, even the ancestors of the Khor. Earth is the world of men."

"How do you know all this?" demanded Zap 210.

"Sometime I'll tell you. Not tonight."

They set off across the downs, walking through the starry night, and something about the circumstances put Reith in a strange frame of mind. It was as if he were young and roaming a starlit meadow of Earth with a slim girl with whom he had become infatuated. So strong became the dream, or the hallucination, or whatever the nature of his mood, that he groped out for Zap 210's hand, where she trudged beside him. She turned him a wan uncomplaining glance, but made no protest: here was another incomprehensible aspect of the astounding *ghaun.*

* Later Reith learned more of the sacred groves, and the Khor intersocial relationships. In the towns and villages, men and women wore identical clothes; sexual activity was regarded as unnatural conduct. Only in the sacred groves, with nudity and the ritual masks to emphasize sexual disparity, did procreation occur. Men and woman, in assuming the masks, assumed new personalities; children were regarded not as the issue of specific parents, but as the yield of archetypal Man and Woman.

So they went on for a period. Reith gradually recovered his senses. He walked the surface of Tschai; his companion— He left the thought incomplete, for a variety of reasons. As if she had sensed the alteration of his mood Zap 210 angrily snatched away her hand; perhaps for a space of time she had been dreaming as well.

They marched on in silence. At last, with the blue moon hanging directly above, they reached the sandstone promontory, and found a protected niche at the base. Wrapping themselves in their cloaks, they huddled upon a drift of sand. . . . Reith could not sleep. He lay looking up at the sky and listening to the sound of the girl's breathing. Like himself, she lay awake. Why had he felt so urgently compelled to flee the Khor grove at the risk of pursuit and death? To protect the girl's innocence? Ridiculous. He looked to find her face, a pale blotch in the moonlight, turned in his direction.

"I can't sleep," she said in a soft voice. "I am too tired. The surface frightens me."

"Sometimes it frightens me," said Reith. "Still, would you rather be back in the Shelters?"

As always she made a tangential response. "I can't understand what I see; I can't understand myself. . . . Never have I heard such singing."

"They sang songs which never change," said Reith. "Songs perhaps from old Earth."

"They showed themselves without clothes! Is this how the surface people act?"

"Not all of them," said Reith.

"But why do they act that way?"

Sooner or later, thought Reith, she must learn the processes of human biology. Not tonight, not tonight! "Nakedness doesn't mean much," he mumbled. "Everyone has a body much like everyone else's."

"But why should they wish to show themselves? In the Shelters we remain covered, and try to avoid 'boisterous conduct.' "

"Just what is this 'boisterous conduct'?"

"Vulgar intimacy. People touch other people and play with them. It's all quite ridiculous."

Reith chose his words with care. "This is probably normal human conduct—like becoming hungry, or something of the sort. You've never been 'boisterous'?"

"Of course not!"

"You've never even thought about it?"

"One can't help thinking."

"Hasn't there ever been a young man with whom you've especially wanted to be friendly?"

"Never!" Zap 210 was scandalized.

"Well, you're on the surface and things may be different. . . . Now you'd better go to sleep. Tomorrow there may be a townful of Khors chasing us."

Reith finally slept. He awoke once to find the blue moon gone, the sky dark except for constellations. From far across the downs came the sad hooting of a night-hound. When he settled back into his cloak Zap 210 said in a drowsy whisper: "The sky frightens me."

Reith moved close beside her; involuntarily, or so it seemed, he reached out and stroked her head, where the hair was now soft and thick. She sighed and relaxed, arousing in Reith an embarrassed protectiveness.

The night passed. A russet glow appeared in the east, waxing to become a lilac and honey-colored dawn. While Zap 210 sat huddled in her cloak, Reith investigated the pouches he had taken from the Khors. He was pleased to find sequins to the value of ninety-five: more than he had expected. He discarded the darts, needle-sharp iron bolts eight inches long with a leather tail; the dagger he tucked into his belt.

They set out up the slopes of the promontory, and presently gained the ridge. Carina 4269, rising at their backs, shone along the shore, revealing another sweep of low beach and mud flats, with far off another promontory like the one on which they stood. The Khor town occupied a hillside slope a mile to the left. Almost at their feet a pier zigzagged across the mud flats and out into the sea: a precarious construction of

poles, rope and planks, vibrating to the current which
swirled around the base of the promontory. Half a
dozen boats were moored to the spindly piles: double-
ended craft, high at bow and stern like sway-backed
dories fitted with masts. Reith looked toward the town.
A few plumes of smoke rose from the black iron roofs;
otherwise no activity was perceptible. Reith turned
back to his inspection of the boats.

"It's easier to sail than to walk," Reith told Zap
210. "And there seems to be a fair wind up the coast."

Zap 210 spoke in consternation: "Out across so
much emptiness?"

"The emptier the better," said Reith. "The sea gives
me no worry; it's the folk who sail there. . . . The
same is just as true of the land, of course." He set off
down the slope; Zap 210 scrambled after him. They
reached the end of the pier and started along the rick-
ety walkway. From somewhere nearby came a shriek
of anger. They saw a half-grown boy racing toward the
village.

Reith broke into a run. "Come along, hurry! We
won't have much time."

Zap 210 came panting behind him. The two reached
the end of the pier. "We won't be able to escape!
They'll follow us in the boats."

"No," said Reith. "I think not." He looked from
boat to boat, and chose that which seemed the most
staunch. In front of the village excited black shapes
had gathered; a dozen started at a run for the pier, followed by as many more.

"Jump down into the boat," said Reith. "Hoist the
sail!"

"It is too late," cried Zap 210. "We will never escape."

"It's not too late. Hoist the sail!"

"I don't know how."

"Pull the rope that goes up over the mast."

Zap 210 clambered down into the boat and tried to
follow Reith's instruction. Reith meanwhile ran along
the pier cutting loose the other boats. Riding the cur-

rent, pushed by the offshore breeze, they drifted away from the dock.

Reith returned to where Zap 210 fumbled desperately with the halyard. She strained with all her might and succeeded in fouling the long yard under the forestay. Reith took a last look toward the screaming villagers, then jumped down into the boat and cast off.

No time to sort out halyards or clear the yard; Reith took up the sweeps, fitted them between the thole pins and put way on the boat. Along the trembling pier surged the screaming Khors. Halting, they whirled their darts; up and out flew a volley of iron, to strike into the water an uncomfortable ten or twenty feet short of the boat. With renewed energy Reith worked the sweeps, then went to hoist the sail. The yard swung free, creaked aloft; the gray sail billowed; the boat heeled and churned through the water. The Khors stood silent on the deck, watching after their departing boats.

Reith sailed directly out to sea. Zap 210 sat huddled in the center of the boat. Finally she made a dispirited protest. "Is it wise to go so far from the land?"

"Very wise. Otherwise the Khors might follow along the shore and kill us when we put into land."

"I have never known such openness. It is exposed—frightfully so."

"On the other hand, our condition is better than it was yesterday at this time. Are you hungry?"

"Yes."

"See what's in that caddy yonder. We may be in luck."

Zap 210 climbed forward to the locker in the bow, where among scraps of rope and gear, spare sails, a lantern, she found a jug of water and a sack of dry pilgrim-pod cakes.

With the shore at last a blur, Reith swung the boat into the northwest, trimming the ungainly sail to the wind.

All day the fair wind blew. Reith held a course ten miles offshore, well beyond the scope of Khor vision.

Headlands appeared in the murk of distance, loomed
off the beam, slowly dwindled and disappeared.

As the afternoon waned the wind increased, sending
whitecaps chasing over the dark sea. The rigging
creaked, the sails bulged, the boat threw up a bow-
wave, the wake gurgled, and Reith rejoiced at every
mile so swiftly put astern.

Carina 4269 sank behind the mainland hills; the
wind died and the boat lost way. Darkness came; Zap
210 crouched fearfully on the center seat, oppressed by
the expanse of the sky. Reith lost patience with her
fears. He lowered the yard halfway down the mast,
lashed the rudder, made himself as comfortable as possible and slept.

A cool early morning breeze awoke him. Stumbling
about in the pre-dawn gloom he managed to hoist the
yard; then went aft to the tiller, where he steered half-
dozing until the sun arose.

About noon a finger of land thrust forth into the sea;
Reith landed the boat on a dismal gray beach and went
out foraging. He found a brackish stream, a thicket of
dark red dragon-berries, a supply of the ubiquitous pilgrim-pod. In the stream he noticed a number of crusta-
cean-like creatures, but could not bring himself to
catch them.

During the middle afternoon they once again put out
to sea, Reith using the sweeps to pull the boat away
from the beach. They rounded the headland to find a
changed landscape shoreward. The gray beaches and
mud flats had become a narrow fringe of shingle; beyond were barren red cliffs, and Reith, wary of the lee
shore, put well out to sea.

An hour before sunset a long low vessel appeared
over the northeast horizon, faring on the course paral-
lel to their own. With the sun low in the northwest
Reith hoped to evade the attention of those aboard the
ship, which held a sinister resemblance to the pirate
galleys of the Draschade. Hoping to draw away, he altered course to the south. The ship likewise altered
course, coincidentally or not Reith could not be sure.

He swung the boat directly toward the shore, now about ten miles distant; the ship again seemed to alter course. With a sinking heart Reith saw that they must surely be overtaken. Zap 210 watched with sagging shoulders; Reith wondered what he should do if the galley in fact overtook them. She had no knowledge of what to expect: now was hardly the time to explain to her. Reith decided that he would kill her in the event that capture became certain. Then he changed his mind: they would plunge over the side of the boat and drown together. . . . Equally impractical; while there was life there was hope.

The sun settled upon the horizon; the wind, as on the previous evening, lessened. Sunset brought a dead calm with the boats rolling helplessly on the waves.

Reith shipped the sweeps. As twilight settled over the ocean he pulled away from the becalmed pirate ship toward shore. He rowed on through the night. The pink moon rose and then the blue moon, to project tremulous trails across the water.

Ahead, one of the trails ended at a mass of dead black: the shore. Reith stopped his rowing. Far to the west he saw a flickering light; to sea all was dark. He threw out the anchor and lowered the sail. The two made a meal on berries and pilgrim-pod, then lay down to sleep on the sails in the bottom of the boat.

With morning came a breeze from the east. The boat lay at anchor a hundred yards offshore, in water barely three feet deep. The pirate galley, if such it was, could no longer be seen. Reith pulled up the anchor and hoisted sail; the boat moved jauntily off through the water.

Made cautious by the events of the previous afternoon, Reith sailed only a quarter of a mile offshore, until the wind died, halfway through the afternoon. In the north a bank of clouds gave portent of a storm; taking up the sweeps, Reith worked the boat into a lagoon at the mouth of a sluggish river. To the side of the lagoon floated a raft of dried reeds, upon which two boys sat fishing. After an initial stir they watched the approach of the boat in attitudes of indifference.

Reith paused in his rowing to consider the situation. The unconcern of the boys seemed unnatural. On Tschai unusual events almost always presaged danger. Reith cautiously rowed the boat to within conversational distance. A hundred feet distant on the bank sat three men, also fishing. They seemed to be Grays: a people short and stocky, with strongly-featured faces, sparse brownish hair and grayish skin. At least, thought Reith, they were not Khors, and not automatically hostile.

Reith let the boat drift forward. He called out: "Is there a town nearby?"

One of the boys pointed across the reeds to a grove of purple ouinga trees. "Yonder."

"What town is it?"

"Zsafathra."

"Is there an inn or a tavern where we can find accommodation?"

"Speak to the men ashore."

Reith urged the boat toward the bank. One of the men called out in irritation: "Easy with the tumult! You'll drive off every gobbulch in the lagoon."

"Sorry," said Reith. "Can we find accommodation in your town?"

The men regarded him with impersonal curiosity. "What do you here, along this coast?"

"We are travelers, from the south of Kislovan, now returning home."

"You have traveled a remarkable distance in so small a craft," remarked one of the men in a mildly skeptical voice.

"One which strongly resembles the craft of the Khors," noted another.

"For a fact," Reith agreed, "it does look like a Khor boat. But all this aside, what of lodging?"

"Anything is available to folk with sequins."

"We can pay reasonable charges."

The oldest of the men on the bank rose to his feet.

"If nothing else," he stated, "we are a reasonable people." He signaled Reith to approach. As the boat nosed into the reeds he jumped aboard. "So, then: you claim to be Khors?"

"Quite the reverse. We claim not to be Khors."

"What of the boat, then?"

Reith made an ambiguous gesture. "It is not as good as some, but better than others; it has brought us this far."

A wintry grin crossed the man's face. "Proceed through the channel yonder. Bear to the right."

For half an hour Reith rowed this way and that through a maze of channels with the ouinga trees always behind islands of black reeds. Reith presently understood that the Zsafathran either was having a joke or sought to confuse him. He said, "I am tired; you row the rest of the way."

"No, no," declared the old man. "We are now there, just left through yonder channel, and toward the ouingas."

"Odd," said Reith. "We have gone back and forth past that channel a dozen times."

"One channel looks much like another. And here we are."

The boat floated into a placid pond, surrounded by reed-thatched cottages on stilts under the ouinga trees. At the far end of the pond stood a larger, more elaborate structure. The poles were purple ouinga wood; the thatch was woven in a complicated pattern of black, brown and gray.

"Our community free-house," explained the Zsafathran. "We are not so isolated as you might think. Thangs come by with their troupes and carts, or Bihasu peddlers, or wandering dignitaries like yourselves. All these we entertain at our free-house."

"Thangs? We must be close upon Cape Braise!"

"Is three hundred miles close? The Thangs are as pervasive as sand-flies; they appear everywhere, more often than not when they are not wanted. Not too far is the great Thang town Urmank. . . . You and your woman both are of a race strange to me. If the concept were not inherently ludicrous—but no, to postulate nonsense is to lose my dignity; I will hazard nothing."

"We are from a remote place," said Reith. "You have never heard of it."

The old man made a sign of indifference. "Whatever you like; provided that you observe the ceremonies, and pay your score."

"Two questions," said Reith. "What are the 'ceremonies,' and how much must we expect to pay as a daily charge?"

"The ceremonies are simple," said the Zsafathran. "An exchange of pleasantries, so to speak. The charges will be perhaps four or five sequins a day. Go ashore at the dock, if you will; then we must take your boat away, to discourage speculation should a Thang or a Bihasu pass by."

Reith decided to make no objection. He worked the boat to the dock, a construction of withe and reeds lashed to piles of ouinga-wood. The Zsafathran jumped from the boat, and gallantly helped Zap 210 to the dock, inspecting her closely as he did so.

Reith jumped ashore with a mooring line, which the Zsafathran took and passed on to a lad with a set of muttered instructions. He led Reith and Zap 210 through the withe pavilion and into the great free-house. "So here you are, take your ease. The cubicle yonder is at your service. Food and wine will be served in due course."

"We want to bathe," said Reith, "and we would appreciate a change of clothes if any such are available."

"The bathhouse is yonder. Fresh garments after the Zsafathran style can be furnished at a price."

"And the price?"

"Ordinary suits of gray furze for withe-cutting or tillage are ten sequins each. Since your present garments are little better than rags, I recommend the expense."

"Under-linen is included in this price?"

"Upon a surcharge of two sequins apiece under-linen

is furnished, and should you wish new sandals, each must pay five sequins additionally."

"Very well," said Reith. "Bring everything. We'll go first-class while the sequins last."

Chapter 6

Wearing the simple gray smock and trousers of the Zsafathrans, Zap 210 looked somewhat less peculiar and conspicuous. Her black hair had begun to curl; exposure to wind and sun had darkened her skin; only her perfectly regular features and her brooding absorption with secret ideas now set her apart. Reith doubted, however, if a stranger would notice in her conduct anything more unusual than shyness.

But Cauch, the old Zsafathran, noticed. Taking Reith aside, he muttered in a confidential voice, "Your woman: perhaps she is ill? If you require herbs, sweat-baths or homeopathy, these are available, at no great cost."

"Everything at Zsafathran is a bargain," said Reith. "Before we leave we might owe more sequins than we carry. In this case, what would be your attitude?"

"Sorrowful resignation, nothing more. We know ourselves for a destiny-blasted race, doomed to a succession of disappointments. But I trust this is not to be the case?"

"Not unless we enjoy your hospitality longer than I presently plan."

"No doubt you will carefully gauge your resources. But again, what of the woman's condition?" He subjected Zap 210 to a critical scrutiny. "I have had some experience in these matters; I deem her peaked and listless, and somewhat morose. Beyond this, I am puzzled."

"She is an unfathomable person," Reith agreed.

"The description, if I may say so, applies to you

both," said Cauch. He turned his owlish gaze upon Reith. "Well, the woman's morbidity is your affair, of course. . . . A collation has been served on the pavilion, which you are invited to join."

"At a small charge, presumably?"

"How can it be otherwise? In this exacting world only the air we breathe is free. Are you the sort to go hungry because you begrudge the outlay of a few bice? I think not. Come." And Cauch, urging them out upon the pavilion, seated them in withe chairs before a wicker table, then went off to instruct the girls who served from the buffet.

Cool tea, spice-cakes, stalks of a crisp red water-vegetable were set before them as a first course. The food was palatable, the chairs were comfortable; after the vicissitudes of the previous weeks the situation seemed unreal, and Reith was unable to subdue a nervous mannerism of looking warily this way and that. Gradually he relaxed. The pavilion seemed an idyll of peace. Gauzy fronds of the purple ouinga trailed low, exhaling an aromatic scent. Carina 4269 sprinkled dancing spots of dark gold light across the water. From somewhere beyond the free-house came the music of water-gongs. Zap 210 gazed across the pond in a reverie, nibbling at the food as if it lacked flavor. Becoming aware of Reith's attention she straightened primly in the chair.

"Shall I serve more of this tea?" asked Reith.

"If you like."

Reith poured from the bubble-glass jug. "You don't seem particularly hungry," he observed.

"I suppose not. I wonder if they have any *diko*."

"I'm sure that they have no *diko*," said Reith.

Zap 210 gave her fingers a petulant twitch.

Reith asked, "Do you like this place?"

"It is better than the vastness of the sea."

For a period Reith sipped his tea in silence. The table was cleared; new dishes were set before them: croquettes in sweet jelly; toasted sticks of white pith; nubbins of gray sea-flesh. As before Zap 210 showed no great appetite. Reith said politely, "You've seen something of the surface now. Is it different from your expectations?"

Zap 210 reflected. "I never thought to see so many mother-women," she murmured, as if talking to herself.

" 'Mother-women'? Do you mean women with children?"

She flushed. "I mean the women with prominent breasts and hips. There are so many! Some of them seem very young: no more than girls."

"It's quite normal," said Reith. "As girls grow out of childhood, they develop breasts and hips."

"I am not a child," Zap 210 declared in an unusually haughty voice. "And I . . ." Her voice dwindled away.

Reith poured another mug of tea and settled back into his chair. "It's time," he said, "that I explained certain matters to you. I suppose I should have done so before. All women are 'mother-women.' "

Zap 210 stared at him incredulously. "This isn't the case at all!"

"Yes, it is," said Reith. "The Pnume fed you drugs to keep you immature: the *diko,* or so I imagine. You aren't drugged now and you're becoming normal—more or less. Haven't you noticed changes in yourself?"

Zap 210 sank back in her chair, dumbfounded by his knowledge of her embarrassing secret. "Such things are not to be talked about."

"So long as you know what's happening."

Zap 210 sat looking out over the water. In a diffident voice she asked, "You have noticed changes in me?"

"Well, yes. First of all, you no longer look like the ghost of a sick boy."

Zap 210 whispered, "I don't want to be a fat animal, wallowing in the dark. Must I be a mother?"

"All mothers are women," Reith explained, "but not all women are mothers. Not all mothers become fat animals."

"Strange, strange! Why are some women mothers and not others? Is it evil destiny?"

"Men are involved in the process," said Reith. "Look yonder, on the deck of that cottage: two children, a woman, a man. The woman is a mother. She is young and looks healthy. The man is the father. Without fathers, there are no children."

Before Reith could proceed with his explanation, old Cauch returned to the table and seated himself.

"All is satisfactory?"

"Very much so," said Reith. "We will regret leaving your village."

Cauch nodded complacently. "In a few poor ways we are a fortunate folk, neither rigorous like the Khors, nor obsessively flexible like the Thangs to the west. What of yourselves? I admit to curiosity regarding your provenance and your destination, for I regard you as unusual folk."

Reith ruminated a moment or two, then said: "I don't mind satisfying your curiosity if you are willing to pay my not-unreasonable fee. In fact I can offer you various grades of enlightenment. For a hundred sequins I guarantee amazement and awe."

Cauch drew back, hands raised in protest. "Tell me nothing upon which you place a value! But any oddments of small talk you can spare at no charge will find in me an attentive listener."

Reith laughed. "Triviality is a luxury I can't afford. Tomorrow we depart Zsafathra. Our few sequins must take us to Sivishe—in what fashion I don't know."

"As to this I can't advise you," said Cauch, "not even for a fee. My experience extends only so far as Urmank. Here you must go carefully. The Thangs will take all your sequins without a qualm. Useless to feel anger or injury! This is the Thang temperamant. Rather than work they prefer to connive; Zsafathrans are very much on their guard when they visit Urmank, as you will see should you choose to go in our company to the Urmank bazaar."

"Hmm." Reith rubbed his chin. "What of our boat, in this case?"

Cauch shrugged, somewhat too casually or so it seemed to Reith. "What is a boat? A floating shell of wood."

"We had planned to sell this valuable boat at Urmank," said Reith. "Still, to save myself the effort of navigation, I will let it go here for less than its full value."

With a quiet laugh Cauch shook his head. "I have no need for so clumsy and awkward a craft. The rigging is frayed, the sails are by no means the best; there is only a poor assortment of gear and rope in the forward caddy."

After an hour and a half of proposals and counterproposals Reith disposed of the boat for forty-two sequins, together with all costs of accommodation at Zsafathra, and transportation to Urmank on the morrow. As they bargained they consumed quantities of the pepper tea, a mild intoxicant. Reith's mood became loose and easy. The present seemed none too bad. The future? It would be met on its own terms. At the moment the failing afternoon light seeped through the enormous ouinga trees, pervading the air with dusty violet, and the pond mirrored the sky.

Cauch went off about his affairs; Reith leaned back in his chair. He considered Zap 210, who also had drunk a considerable quantity of the pepper tea. Some alteration of his mood caused him to see her not as a Pnumekin and a freak but as a personable young woman sitting quietly in the dusk. Her attention was fixed on something across the pavilion; what she saw astonished her and she turned to Reith in wonder. Reith noticed how large and dark were her eyes. She spoke in a shocked whisper. "Did you see . . . *that?*"

"What?"

"A young man and a young woman—they stood close and put their faces together!"

"Really!"

"Yes!"

"I can't believe it. Just what did they do?"

"Well—I can't quite describe it."

"Was it like this?" Reith put his hands on her shoulders, looked deep into the startled eyes.

"No . . . not quite. They were closer."

"Like this?"

Reith put his arms around her. He remembered the cold water of the Pagaz lake, the desperate animal vitality of her body as she had clung to him. "Was it like this?"

She pushed back at his shoulders. "Yes . . . Let me go; someone might think us boisterous."

"Did they do this?" Reith kissed her. She looked at him in astonishment and alarm, and put her hand to her mouth. "No. . . . Why did you do that?"

"Did you mind?"

"Well, no. I don't think so. But please don't do it again; it makes me feel very strangely."

"That," said Reith, "is the effects of the *diko* wearing off." He drew back and sat with his head spinning. She looked at him uncertainly. "I can't understand why you did that."

Reith took a deep breath. "It's natural for men and women to be attracted to each other. This is called the reproductive instinct, and sometimes it results in children."

Zap 210 became alarmed. "Will I now be a mother-woman?"

"No," said Reith. "We'd have to become far friendlier."

"You're sure?"

Reith thought that she leaned toward him. "I'm sure." He kissed her again, and this time, after a first nervous motion, she made no resistance . . . then she gasped. "Don't move. They won't notice us if we sit like this; they'll be ashamed to look."

Reith froze, his face close to hers. "Who won't notice us?" he muttered.

"Look—now."

Reith glanced over his shoulder. Across the pavilion

stood two dark shapes wearing black cloaks and wide-brimmed black hats.

"Gzhindra," she whispered.

Cauch came into the pavilion, and went to talk with the Gzhindra. After a moment he led them out into the road.

Dusk became night. Across the pavilion the serving girls hung up lamps with yellow and green shades, and brought new trays and tureens to the buffet table. Reith and Zap 210 sat somberly back in the shadows.

Cauch, returning to the pavilion, joined them. "Tomorrow at dawn we will depart for Urmank, and no doubt arrive by noon. You know the reputation of the Thangs?"

"To some extent."

"The reputation is deserved," said Cauch. "They cheat in preference to keeping faith; their favorite money is stolen money. So be on your guard."

Reith asked casually, "Who were the two men in black with whom you spoke half an hour ago?"

Cauch nodded as if he had been awaiting the question. "Those were Gzhindra, or Ground-men as we call them, who sometimes act as agents for the Pnume. Their business tonight was different. They have taken a commission from the Khors to locate a man and woman who desecrated a sacred place and stole a boat near the town Fauzh. The description, by a peculiar coincidence, matched your own, though certain discrepancies enabled me to state with accuracy that no such persons had been seen at Zsafathra. Still they may discuss the matter with people who do not know you as well as I; to avoid any possible confusion of identities, I suggest that you alter your appearance as dramatically as possible."

"That is easier said than done," said Reith.

"Not altogether." Cauch put his fingers into his mouth producing a shrill whistle. Without surprise or haste one of the serving girls approached: a pleasant creature, broad in hips, shoulders, cheekbones and mouth, with nondescript brown hair worn in a wildly coquettish array of ringlets. "Well, then, you desire something?"

"Bring a pair of turbans," said Cauch. "The orange and white, with black bangles."

The girl procured the articles. Going to Zap 210, she wound the orange and white cloth around the black cap of hair, tied it so that the tasseled ends hung behind the left ear, then affixed black bangles to swing somewhat in front of the right ear. Reith marveled at the transformation. Zap 210 now seemed daring and mischievous, a gay young girl costumed as a pirate.

Reith was next fitted with the turban; Zap 210 seemed to find the transformation amusing; she opened her mouth and laughed: the first occasion Reith had heard her do so.

Cauch appraised them both. "A remarkable difference. You have become a pair of Hedaijhans. Tomorrow I will provide you with shawls. Your very mothers would not know you."

"What do you charge for this service?" demanded Reith. "A reasonable sum, I hope?"

"A total of eight sequins, to include the articles themselves, fitting, and training in the postures of the Hedaijhans. Essentially, you must walk with a swagger, swinging your arms—so." Cauch demonstrated a mincing lurching gait. "With your hands—so. Now, lady, you first. Remember, your knees must be bent. Swing, swagger. . . ."

Zap 210 followed the instructions with great earnestness, looking toward Reith to see if he laughed.

The practice went on into the night, while the pink moon sailed behind the ouinga trees, and the blue moon rose in the east. Finally Cauch pronounced himself satisfied. "You would deceive almost anyone. So then, to the couch. Tomorrow we journey to Urmank."

The sleeping cubicle was dim, cracks in the rattan wall admitting slits of green and yellow light from the pavilion lamps, as many more from the pink and blue

moons shining from different directions to make a mul-
ticolored mesh on the floor.

Zap 210 went to the wall and peered through the
cracks out toward the avenue which ran under the
ouingas. She looked for several minutes. Reith came to
join her. "What do you see?"

"Nothing. They would not let themselves be seen so
easily." She turned away and with an inscrutable
glance toward Reith went to sit on one of the wicker
couches. Presently she said, "You are a very strange
man."

Reith had no reply to make.

"There is so much you don't tell me. Sometimes I
feel as if I know nothing whatever."

"What do you want to know?"

"How people of the surface act, how they feel . . .
why they do the things they do. . . ."

Reith went to where she sat and stood looking down
at her. "Do you want to learn all these things tonight?"

She sat looking down at her hands. "No. I'm
afraid. . . . Not now."

Reith reached out and touched her head. He was
suddenly wildly tempted to sit down beside her and tell
her the tale of his remarkable past. . . . He wanted to
feel her eyes on him; to see her pale face attentive and
marveling. . . . In fact, thought Reith, he had begun
to find this strange girl with her secret thoughts stimu-
lating.

He turned away. As he crossed to his own couch he
felt her eyes on his back.

Chapter 7

The morning sunlight entered the cubicle, strained by the withes of the wall. Going out upon the pavilion, Reith and Zap 210 found Cauch making a breakfast of pilgrim-pod cakes and a hot broth redolent of the shore. He inspected Reith and Zap 210 narrowly, paying particular attention to the turbans and their gait. "Not too bad. But you tend to forget. More swagger, lady, more shrug to your shoulders. Remember when you leave the pavilion you are Hedaijhans! In case suspicions have been aroused, in case someone waits and watches."

After breakfast, the three went out upon the avenue which led northward under the ouinga trees, Reith and Zap 210 as thoroughly Hedaijhan as turban, shawl and mincing gait could make them, to a pair of carts drawn by a type of animal Reith had not previously seen: a gray-skinned beast which pranced elegantly and precisely on eight long legs.

Cauch climbed aboard the first cart; Reith and Zap 210 joined him. The carts departed Zsafathra.

The road led out upon a damp land of reeds, water-plants, isolated black stumps trailing lime-green tendrils. Cauch gave a great deal of his attention to the sky, as did the Zsafathrans in the cart behind. Reith finally asked: "What are you watching for?"

"Occasionally," said Cauch, "we are molested by a tribe of predatory birds from the hills yonder. In fact, there you see one of their sentinels." He pointed to a black speck flapping across the southern sky; it appeared the size of a large buzzard. Cauch went on in a voice of resignation. "Presently they will fly out to attack us."

"You show no great alarm," said Reith.

"We have learned how to deal with them." Cauch turned and gestured to the cart behind, then accelerated the pace of his own cart, to open up a gap of a hundred yards between the two. Out of the southern skies came a flock of fifty or sixty flapping bird-creatures. As they drew near Reith saw that each carried two chunks of stone half the size of his head. He looked uneasily toward Cauch. "What do they do with the rocks?"

"They drop them, with remarkable accuracy. Assume that you stood in the road, and that thirty creatures flew above you at their customary height of five hundred feet. Thirty stones would strike you and crush you to the ground."

"Evidently you have learned how to frighten them off."

"No, nothing of the sort."

"You disturb their accuracy?"

"To the contrary. We are essentially a passive people and we try to deal with our enemies so that they disconcert or defeat themselves. Have you wondered why the Khors do not attack us?"

"The thought has occurred to me."

"When the Khors attack—and they have not done so for six hundred years—we evade them and by one means or another penetrate their sacred groves. Here we perform acts of defilement, of the most simple, natural and ordinary sort. They no longer can use the grove for procreation and must either migrate or perish. Our weapons, I agree, are indelicate, but typify our philosophy of warfare."

"And these birds?" Reith dubiously watched the approach of the flock. "Surely the same weapons are ineffectual?"

"I would presume so," Cauch agreed, "though for a

fact we have never tested them. In this case we do nothing whatever."

The birds soared overhead; Cauch urged the dray-beast into a sinuous lope. One by one the birds dropped their stones, which fell to strike the road behind the cart.

"The birds, you must understand, can only compute the position of a stationary target; in this case their accuracy is their undoing."

The stones were all dropped; with croaks of frustration the birds flew back to the mountains. "They will more than likely return with another load of stones," said Cauch. "Do you notice how this road is elevated some four feet above the surrounding marsh? The toil has been accomplished by the birds over many centuries. They are dangerous only if you stand to watch."

The carts moved through a forest of wax-brown trees, seething with hordes of small white fuzz-balls, half-spider, half-monkey, which bounded from branch to branch, venting raucous little screams and hurling twigs at the travelers. The road then led twenty miles across a plain littered with boulders of honey-colored tuff, toward a pair of tall volcanic necks, each growing into an ancient weathered castle, in ages past the headquarters of hermetic cults but now, according to Cauch, the abode of ghouls. "By day they are never seen, but by night they come down to prowl the outskirts of Urmank. Sometimes the Thangs catch them in traps for use at the carnival."

The road passed between the peaks and Urmank came into view: a disorderly straggle of high, narrow houses of black timber, brown tile and stone. A quay bordered the waterfront, where half a dozen ships floated placidly at moorages. Behind the quay was the marketplace and bazaar, to which a flutter of orange and green banners gave a festive air. A long wall of crumbling brick bounded the bazaar; a clutter of mud huts beyond seemed to indicate a caste of pariahs.

"Behold Urmank!" said Cauch. "The town of the Thangs. They are not fastidious as to who comes and who goes, provided only that they take away fewer sequins than they brought."

"In my case they will be disappointed," said Reith. "I hope to gain sequins, by one means or another."

Cauch gave him a marveling side-glance. "You intend to take sequins from the Thangs? If you control such a miraculous power please share it with me. The Thangs have cheated us so regularly that now they regard the process as their birthright. Oh, I tell you, in Urmank you must be wary!"

"If you are cheated, why do you deal with them?"

"It seems an absurdity," Cauch admitted. "After all, we could build a ship and sail it to Hedaijha, the Green Erges, Coad—but we are a wry people; it amuses us to come to Urmank where the Thang provide entertainments. Look yonder; see the area wrapped around with brown and orange canvas? There is the site of the stilting. Beyond are the games of chance, where the visitor invariably loses more than he gains. Urmank is a challenge to Zsafathra; always we hope to outwit the Thangs."

"Our joint efforts may yield a profit," said Reith. "At least I can bring a fresh outlook to bear."

Cauch gave an indifferent shrug. "Zsafathrans have tried to outdo the Thangs from beyond the brink of memory. They deal with us by formula. First we are enticed by the prospect of quick gain; then after we have put down our sequins the prospects recede. . . . Well, first we will refresh ourselves. The Inn of the Lucky Mariner has proved satisfactory in the past. As my associate you are safe from thuggery, kidnap and slave-taking. However, you must guard your own money; the Thangs can be coerced only so far and no further."

The common room at the Inn of the Lucky Mariner was furnished in a style Reith had not seen previously on Tschai. Angular chairs of wooden posts and poles lined the walls, which were white-washed brick. In alcoves glass pots displayed the movement of iridescent sea-worms. The chief functionary wore a brown kaftan buttoned down the front, a black skullcap, black slippers and black finger-guards. His face was bland, his manners suave; he proffered for Reith's inspection a pair of adjoining cubicles furnished with couch, nightstand and lamp, which, with fresh body linen and foot ointment, rented for the inclusive sum of three sequins. Reith thought the figure reasonable and said as much to Cauch.

"Yes," said Cauch. "Three sequins is no great amount, but I recommend that you make no use of the foot ointment. As a new amenity, it arouses suspicion. It may stain the woodwork, whereupon you will be levied an extra charge. Or it may contain a pulsing vesicant, the balm for which sells at five sequins the dram."

Cauch spoke in full earshot of the functionary, who laughed quietly and without offense. "Old Zsafathran, you are over-skeptical for once. Recently we were required to accept a large stock of tonics and ointments in lieu of payment, and we have merely put these substances at the disposal of our guests. Do you require a diuretic or a vermifuge? We supply these at only a nominal charge."

"At the moment, nothing," said Cauch.

"What of your Hedaijhan friends? Everyone is the better for an occasional purge, which we offer at ten bice. No? Well then, for your evening meal let me recommend The Choicest Offerings of Land and Sea a few steps to the right along the quay."

"I have dined there on a previous occasion," said Cauch. "The substances set before me would have quelled the appetite of a High-castle ghoul. We will buy bread and fruit in the market."

"In that case, be so good as to patronize the booth of my nephew, opposite the depilatorium!"

"We will inspect his produce." Cauch led the way out upon the quay. "The Lucky Mariner's comparatively scrupulous; still, as you see, one must be alert. On my last visit, a troupe of musicians played in the common room. I stopped for a moment to listen and on my reckoning discovered a charge of four sequins. And as far as the offer of purgative at little or no charge"—here Cauch coughed—"this is all very well. On a previous visit to Urmank a similar offer was put to my grandfather, who accepted and thereafter discovered a lock on the door to the convenience, and a consequent usage charge. The medication, in the long run, cost him dearly. It is wise in one's dealings with the Thangs to examine every aspect of a situation."

The three strolled along the quay, Reith examining the ships with interest. These were all fat-bellied little cogs, with high poops and foredecks, propelled by sails when the wind was fair and an electric jet-pump otherwise. In front of each a board announced the name of the ship, the port of destination and the date of sailing.

Cauch touched Reith's arm. "It might be imprudent to evince too great an interest in the ships."

"Why?"

"At Urmank it is always the part of wisdom to dissemble."

Reith looked back up the quay. "No one appears to be heeding us. If they are, they will take it for granted that I dissemble and actually plan a journey overland."

Cauch sighed. "At Urmank life has many surprises for the unwary."

Reith halted by a board. "The ship *Nhiahar*. Destinuation: Ching, the Murky Isles, the South Schanizade Coast, Kazain. A moment." Reith climbed a gangplank and approached a thin and somber man in a leather apron.

"Where is the captain, if you please?"

"I am he."

"In connection with a voyage to Kazain: what fare would you demand for two persons?"

"For the Class A cabin I require four sequins per person per diem, which includes nutrition. The passage to Kazain is generally thirty-two days; hence the total fee for two persons is, let us say, two hundred and sixty sequins."

Reith expressed surprise at the magnitude of the

amount, but the captain maintained an indifferent attitude.

Reith returned to the dock. "I need something over two hundred and fifty sequins."

"Not an impossible sum," said Cauch. "A diligent laborer can earn four or even six sequins a day. Porters are always in demand along the docks."

"What of the gambling booths?"

"The district is yonder, beside the bazaar. Needless to say, you are unlikely to overcome the Thang gamesters on their own premises."

They walked into a plaza paved with squares of salmon-pink stone. "A thousand years ago the tyrant Przelius built a great rotunda here. Only a floor remains. There: food-stalls. There: garments and sandals. There: ointments and extracts . . ." As Cauch spoke he pointed toward various quarters of the plaza, where the booths offered a great variety of goods: foodstuffs, cloth, leather; an earth-colored melange of spices; tinware and copper; black iron slabs, pads, rods and bars; glassware and lamps; paper charms and fetishes. Beyond the floor of the rotunda and the more or less orderly array of booths were the entertainments: orange tents with rugs in front where girls danced to nose-flutes and snap-blocks. Some wore garments of gauze; others danced bare to the waist; a few no more than a year or two from childhood wore only sandals. Zap 210 watched these and their postures with amazement. Then, with a shrug and a numb expression, she turned away.

Muffled chanting attracted Reith's attention. A canvas wall enclosed a small stadium, from which now came a sudden chorus of hoots and groans. "The stilt contests," Cauch explained. "It appears that one of the champions has been downed, and many wagers have gone by the boards."

As they passed the stadium Reith caught a view of four men on ten-foot stilts stalking warily around each other. One kicked forth with his stilt; another struck a blow with a pillow-headed club; a third caught unaware careened away, preserving his balance by a miracle, while the others hopped after him like grotesque carrion-birds.

"The stilt-fighters are mostly Black Mountain mica-cutters," said Cauch. "The outsider who wagers on the bouts might as well drop his money into a hole." Cauch gave his head a rueful jerk. "Still, we always hope. My brother's name-father won forty-two sequins at the eel-race some years ago. I must admit that for two days previously he burnt incense and implored divine intervention."

"Let's watch an eel-race," said Reith. "If divine intervention earns a profit of forty-two sequins, our own intelligence should produce at least as much and hopefully more."

"This way then, past the brat-house."

Reith was about to inquire what a brat-house might be, when a grinning urchin ran close and kicked Reith on the shins then, dodging back, made an ugly face and ran into the brat-house. Reith looked after the child in wrathful puzzlement. "What's the reason for that?"

"Come," said Cauch. "I'll show you."

He led the way into the brat-house. On a stage thirty feet distant stood the child, who upon their entrance emitted a hideous taunting squeal. Behind the counter stood a suave middle-aged Thang with a silky brown moustache. "Nasty tyke, don't you think? Here, give him a good pelting. These mud-balls come ten bice apiece. The dung-packets are six to the sequin and these prickle-burrs are five to the sequin."

"Yah, yah, yah!" screamed the urchin. "Why worry? He couldn't heave a rock this far!"

"Go ahead, sir, give it to him," suggested the operator. "Which will it be? The mud-balls? The dung-packets make a hideous reek; the brat despises them. And the thorn-balls! He'll rue the day he attacked you."

"You get up there," said Reith. "Let me throw at you."

"Prices double, sir."

Reith departed the brat-house with the taunts of both urchin and operator accompanying him to the reach of earshot.

"Wise restraint," said Cauch. "No sequins to be earned in such a place."

"One can't live by bread alone . . . but no matter. Show me the eel-races."

"Only a few steps further."

They walked toward the sagging old wall which separated the bazaar from Urmank Old Town. At the very edge of the open area, almost in the shadow of the wall, they came to a U-shaped counter surrounded by two-score men and women, many wearing outland garments. A few feet beyond the open end of the U a wooden reservoir stood on a concrete platform. The reservoir, six feet in diameter and two feet high, was equipped with a hinged cover and emptied into a covered flume which ran between the arms of the U, to empty into a glass basin at the far bend. The attention of the players was riveted upon the glass basin; as Reith watched a green eel darted forth from the chute and into the basin, followed after a moment or two by eels of various other colors.

"Green wins again!" cried out the eel-master in a voice of anguish. "Lucky lucky green! Hands behind the screen, please, until I pay the winners! I am sorely hit! Twenty sequins for this Jadarak gentleman, who risked a mere two sequins. Ten sequins for this green-hatted lady of the Azote Coast, who chanced a sequin on the color of her hat! . . . What? No more? Is this all? I have not been struck so sorely as first I feared." The operator cleared the boards of sequins laid down upon the other colors. "A new race will now occur; arrange your bets. Sequins must be placed squarely upon the chosen color, if you please, to avoid misunderstanding. I set no limit; bet as high as you please, up to a limit of a thousand sequins, since my total wealth and reserve is only ten thousand. Five times already I have been bankrupted; always I have climbed back from poverty to serve the gambling folk of Urmank; is this not true dedication?" As he spoke, he gathered the eels into a basket and carried them to the upper end of the chute. He hauled on a rope which, passing over a frame, lifted the lid of the reservoir. Reith edged close and peered down into the pool of water contained within. The eel-master made no objection. "Look your fill, my man; the only mysteries here are the eels themselves. If I could read their secrets I would be a rich man today!" Within the reservoir Reith saw a baffle which defined a spiral channel originating at a center well and twisting out to the chute, with a gate at the center well which the eel-master now snapped shut. Into the center well he placed the eels and closed down the lid. "You have witnessed," he called out. "The eels move at random, as free as though they traveled the depths of their native streams. They whirl, they race, they seek a ray of light; when I raise the gate all will dash forth. Which will win the race to the basin? Ah, who knows? The last winner was Green; will Green win again? Place your bets, all bets down! Aha! A grandee here wagers generously upon Gray and Mauve, ten sequins on each! What's this? A purple sequin upon Purple! Behold, all! A noblewoman of the Bashai backlands wagers a hundred-value on Purple! Will she win a thousand? Only the eels know."

"I know too," Cauch muttered to Reith. "She will not win. Purple eel will loiter along the way. I predict a win for White or Pale Blue."

"Why do you say that?"

"No one has bet on Pale Blue. Only three sequins are down on White."

"True, but how do the eels know?"

"Herein, as the eel-master avers, lies the mystery."

Reith asked Zap 210: "Can you understand how the operator controls the eels to his profit?"

"I don't understand anything."

"We'll have to give this matter some thought," said Reith. "Let's watch another race. In the interests of research I'll put a sequin down upon Pale Blue."

"Are all bets made?" called out the eel-master.

"Please be meticulous! Sequins overlapping two colors are reckoned to fall on the losing color. No more bets? Very well then, please keep hands behind the screen. No more bets, please! The race is about to begin!"

Stepping to the reservoir, he pulled a lever which presumably lifted the gate from in front of the spiral baffle. "The race is in progress! Eels vie for light; they cavort and wheel in their joy! Down the chute they come! Which is to win?"

The gamblers craned their necks to watch; into the basin streaked the White eel. "Ah," groaned the operator. "How can I profit with such uncooperative eels? Twenty sequins to this already wealthy Gray; you are a mariner, sir? And ten to this noble young slave-taker from Cape Braise. I pay, I pay; where is my profit?" He came past, flipping Reith's sequin into his tray. "So then, everyone alert for the next race."

Reith turned to Cauch with a shake of his head. "Perplexing, perplexing indeed. We had better go on."

They wandered the bazaar until Carina 4269 went down the sky. They watched a wheel of fortune; they studied a game where the participants bought a bag of irregular colored tablets and sought to fit them together into a checkerboard; a half-dozen other games, more or less ordinary. Sunset arrived; the three went to a small restaurant near the Inn of the Lucky Mariner, where they dined upon fish in red sauce, pilgrim-pod bread, a salad of sea-greens and a great black flask of wine. "In only one phase of existence," said Cauch, "can the Thang be trusted: their cuisine, to which they are loyal. The reason for this particularity escapes me."

"It goes to demonstrate," said Reith, "that you can't judge a man by the table he sets."

Cauch asked shrewdly, "How then can a man judge his fellows? For example, what is the basis of your calculation?"

"Only one thing I know for certain," said Reith. "First thoughts are always wrong."

Cauch, sitting back, inspected Reith under quizzical eyebrows. "True, quite possibly true. For instance, you probably are not the cool desperado you appear on first meeting."

"I have been judged even more harshly," said Reith. "One of my friends declares that I seem like a man from another world."

"Odd that you should say that," remarked Cauch. "A strange rumor has recently reached Zsafathra, to the effect that all men originated on a far planet, much as the Redeemers of Yao aver, and not from a union of the sacred xyxyl bird and the sea-demon Rhadamth. Furthermore, it was told that certain folk from this far planet now wander Old Tschai, performing the most remarkable deeds: defying the Dirdir, defeating the Chasch, persuading the Wankh. A new feeling is abroad across Tschai: the sense that change is on its way. What do you think of all this?"

"I suppose the rumor is not inherently absurd," said Reith.

Zap 210 said in a subdued voice: "A planet of men: it would be more strange and wild than Tschai!"

"That of course is problematical," remarked Cauch in a voice of didactic analysis, "and no doubt irrelevant to our present case. The secrets of personality are mystifying. For instance, consider the three of us. One honest Zsafathran and two brooding vagabonds driven like leaves before the winds of fate. What prompts such desperate journeys? What is to be gained? I myself in all my lifetime have not gone so far as Cape Braise; yet I feel none the worse, a trifle dull perhaps. I look at you and ponder. The girl is frightened; the man is harsh; goals beyond her understanding propel him; he takes her where she fears to go. Still, would she go back if she could?" Cauch looked into Zap 210's face; she turned away.

Reith managed a painful grin. "Without money we won't go anywhere."

"Bah," said Cauch bluffly, "if money is all you lack, I have the remedy. Once a week, each Ivensday, combat trials are arranged. In point of fact, Otwile the champion sits yonder." He nodded toward a totally bald man almost seven feet tall, massive in the shoulders and thighs, narrow at the hips. He sat alone sipping wine, staring morosely out upon the quay. "Otwile is a great fighter," said Cauch. "He once grappled a Green Chasch buck and held his own; at least he escaped with his life."

"What are the prizes?" Reith inquired.

"The man who remains five minutes within the circle wins a hundred sequins; he is paid a further twenty sequins for each broken bone. Otwile sometimes provides a hundred-worth within the minute."

"And what if the challenger throws Otwile away?"

Cauch pursed his lips. "No prize is posted; the feat is considered impossible. Why do you ask? Do you plan to make the trial?"

"Not I," said Reith. "I need three hundred sequins. Assume that I remained five minutes in the ring to gain a hundred sequins. . . . I would then need ten broken bones to earn a further two hundred."

Cauch seemed disappointed. "You have an alternative scheme?"

"My mind reverts to the eel-race. How can the operator control eleven eels from a distance of ten feet while they swim down a covered chute? It seems extraordinary."

"It does indeed," declared Cauch. "For years folk of Zsafathra have put down their sequins on the presumption that such control is impossible."

"Might the eels alter color to suit the circumstances? Impractical, unthinkable. Does the operator stimulate the eels telepathically? I consider this unlikely."

"I have no better theories," said Cauch.

Reith reviewed the eel-master's procedure. "He raises the lid of the reservoir; the interior is open and visible; the water is no more than a foot deep. The eels are placed into the center well and the lid is closed down: this before betting is curtailed. Yet the eel-master appears to control the motion of the eels."

Cauch gave a sardonic chuckle. "Do you still think you can profit from the eel-races?"

"I would like to examine the premises a second time." Reith rose to his feet.

"Now? The races are over for the day."

"Still, let us examine the ground; it is only five minutes' walk."

"As you wish."

The area surrounding the eel-race layout was deserted and lit dimly by the glow of distant bazaar lamps. After the animation of the daytime hours, the table, reservoir and chute seemed peculiarly silent.

Reith indicated the wall which limited the compound. "What lies to the other side?"

"The Old Town and, beyond, the mausoleums, where the Thangs take their dead—not a place to visit by night."

Reith examined the chute and reservoir, the lid to which was locked down for the night. He turned to Cauch. "What time do the races begin?"

"At noon, precisely."

"Tomorrow morning I'd like to look around some more."

"Indeed," mused Cauch. He looked at Reith sidewise. "You have a theory?"

"A suspicion. If—" He looked around as Zap 210 grasped his arm. She pointed. "Over there."

Across the compound walked two figures in black cloaks and wide black hats.

"Gzhindra," said Zap 210.

Cauch said nervously, "Let us return to the inn. It is not wise to walk the dark places of Urmank."

At the inn Cauch retired to his chamber. Reith took Zap 210 to her cubicle. She was reluctant to enter. "What's the matter?" asked Reith.

"I am afraid."

"Of what?"

"The Gzhindra are following us."

"That's not necessarily true. Those might have been any two Gzhindra."

"But perhaps they weren't."

"In any event they can't get at you in the room."

The girl was still dubious.

"I'm right next door," said Reith. "If anyone bothers you—scream."

"What if someone kills you first?"

"I can't think that far ahead," said Reith. "If I'm dead in the morning, don't pay the score."

She wanted further reassurance. Reith patted the soft black curls. "Good night."

He closed the door and waited until the bolt shot home. Then he went into his own cubicle and, despite Cauch's reassurances, made a careful examination of floor, walls and ceiling. At last, feeling secure, he turned the light down to a glimmer and lay himself upon the couch.

Chapter 8

The night passed without alarm or disturbance. In the morning Reith and Zap 210 breakfasted alone at the café on the quay. The sky was cloudless; the smoky sunlight left crisp black shadows behind the tall houses and glinted on the water of the harbor. Zap 210 seemed less pessimistic than usual, and watched the porters, the hawkers, the sea-men and outlanders with interest. "What do you think of the *ghian* now?" asked Reith.

Zap 210 at once became grave. "The folk act differently from what I expected. They don't run back and forth; they don't seem maddened by the sun-glare. Of course"—she hesitated—"one sees a great deal of boisterous conduct, but no one seems to mind. I marvel at the garments of the girls; they are so bold, as if they want to provoke attention. And again, no one objects."

"Quite the reverse," said Reith.

"I could never act like that," Zap 210 said primly. "That girl coming toward us: see how she walks! Why does she act that way?"

"That's how she's put together. Also, she wants men to notice her. These are the instincts that the *diko* suppressed in you."

Zap 210 protested with unusual fervor: "I eat no *diko* now; I feel no such instincts!"

Reith looked smiling off across the quay. The girl to whom Zap 210 had drawn attention slowed her step, hitched at the orange sash around her waist, smiled at Reith, stared curiously at Zap 210, and sauntered on.

Zap 210 looked sidelong at Reith. She started to

speak, then held her tongue. A moment later she blurted: "I don't understand anything of the *ghian*. I don't understand you. Just now you smiled at that odious girl. You never—" Here she stopped short, then continued in a low voice: "I suppose you blame 'instinct' for your conduct."

Reith became impatient. "The time has come," he said, "to explain the facts of life. Instincts are part of our biological baggage and cannot be avoided. Men and women are different." He went on to explain the processes of reproduction. Zap 210 sat rigid, looking across the water. "So," said Reith, "it's not unnatural that people indulge in this kind of conduct."

Zap 210 said nothing. Her hands, so Reith noticed, were clenched and the knuckles shone white.

She said in a low voice, "The Khors in the sacred grove—is *that* what they were doing?"

"So I suppose."

"And you took me away so I wouldn't see."

"Well, yes. I thought you might be confused."

Zap 210 was silent a moment. "We might have been killed."

Reith shrugged. "I suppose there was a chance."

"And those girls dancing without clothes—they wanted to do *that?*"

"If someone gave them money."

"And everyone on the surface feels this way?"

"Most of them, I should say."

"Do you?"

"Certainly. Sometimes, anyway. Not all the time."

"Then why—" she stuttered. "Then why—" she could not finish. Reith reached out to pat her hand; she snatched it away. "Don't touch me!"

"Sorry. . . . But don't be angry."

"You brought me to this horrible place; you deprived me of life; you pretended to be kind—but all the time you've been planning—*that!*"

"No, no!" cried Reith. "Nothing of the sort! You're quite wrong!"

Zap 210 looked at him with eyebrows coolly raised. "You find me repulsive then?"

Reith threw his hands up in the air. "Of course I don't find you repulsive! In fact—"

"In fact, what?"

Cauch, arriving at the table, provided, for Reith, a welcome interruption. "You spent a comfortable night?"

"Yes," said Reith.

Zap 210 rose to her feet and walked away. Cauch drew a long face. "How have I offended her?"

"She's angry with me," said Reith. "Why—I don't know."

"Isn't this always the case? But soon, for reasons equally unknown, she will again become benign. Meanwhile, I am interested in hearing your ideas in regard to the eel-races."

Reith looked dubiously after Zap 210, who had returned to the Inn of the Lucky Mariner. "Is it safe to leave her alone?"

"Have no fear," said Cauch. "At the inn you and she are known to be under my sponsorship."

"Well, then, to the eel-races."

"You understand that they are not yet in operation? The races do not start till noon."

"So much the better."

Zap 210 had never been so angry. She half-walked half-ran to the inn, through the dim common room to the cubicle where she had spent the night. She entered, furiously shot the bolt and went to sit on the couch. For ten minutes she let her thoughts rage without control. Then she began to cry, silently, tears of frustration and disillusionment welling down her cheeks. She thought of the Shelters: the quiet corridors with the black-robed figures drifting past. In the Shelters no one would provoke her to anger or excitement or any of the other strange emotions which from time to time colored her brain. They would give her *diko* once more. . . . She frowned, trying to recall the flavor of the crisp little wafers. On sudden impulse she rose to her feet, examined herself in the mirror which hung on the side wall. The previous evening she had looked at herself with no great interest; the face which looked back seemed just a face: eyes, nose, mouth, chin. Now she studied herself earnestly. She touched the black hair curling down her forehead, combed it with her fingers, studied the effect. The face which looked back was that of a stranger. She thought of the lithe girl who had regarded Reith with such insolence. She had worn a garment of blue cloth which clung to the figure, different from the shapeless gray smock which Zap 210 now wore. She pulled it off, stood in her white undergown. She turned, studied herself from all angles. A stranger now for certain. What if Reith could see her now: what would he think? . . . The idea of Reith made her furiously angry. He considered her a child, or something even more ignoble: she had no word for the concept. She felt herself with her hands and, staring in the mirror, marveled at the changes which had come over her. . . . Her original scheme of returning to the Shelters dwindled. The *zuzhma kastchai* would give her to the darkness. If by chance she were allowed to keep her life, they would feed her *diko* again. Her lips twitched. No more *diko*.

Well, then, what of Adam Reith, who considered her so repulsive that—her mind refused to complete the train of thought. What was to become of her? She studied herself in the mirror and felt very sorry for the dark-haired girl with thin cheeks and sad eyes who looked back at her. If she ran away from Adam Reith how could she survive? . . . She slipped into her gray smock, but decided against tying the orange cloth around her head. Instead she tied it around her waist as a sash, as she had noticed other girls of Urmank doing. She examined herself in the mirror again and rather liked the effect. What would Adam Reith think?

She opened the door, looked up and down the corridor and ventured forth. The common room was empty but for a squat old woman who scrubbed the

stone floor with a brush and looked up with a sneer.
Zap 210 hastened her pace and went out into the
street. Here she hesitated. She had never been alone
before, and the sensation was frightening, if thrilling.
Crossing to the quay, she watched porters unloading a
cog. Neither her vocabulary nor her stock of ideas contained the equivalent of "quaint" or "picturesque";
nevertheless, she was charmed by the bluff-blown craft
moving gently to the heave of the water. She drew a
deep breath. Freak or not, repulsive or not, she had
never felt so alive before. The *ghaun* was a wild cruel
place—here the *zuzhma kastchai* had not dissem-
bled—but after living in the golden-brown sunlight,
how could anyone choose to return to the Shelters?

She walked along the quay to the café, where somewhat diffidently she looked for Reith. What she would
say to him she had not yet formulated; perhaps she
would sweep to her seat with only a haughty glance to
let him know what she thought of his opinions. . . .
Reith was nowhere to be seen. A sudden terrible fear
came over her. Had he taken the opportunity to escape, to be rid of her? Impulses urged upon her; she
wanted to cry out: "Adam Reith! Adam Reith!" She
could not believe that the reassuring form, so taut and
economical of motion, was nowhere to be seen. . . .
She turned to leave and stepped full into the advancing
body of a tall massive man, wearing pantaloons of dove
brown leather, a loose white shirt and a vest of maroon
brocade. A small brimless cap clung to the side of his
bald head; he gave a soft grunt as she walked into him
and held her away with two hands on her shoulders.
"Where do you go in such haste?"

"Nowhere," stammered Zap 210. "I was looking for
someone."

"You have found me, which is not the worst of luck.
Come along; I have not yet had my morning wine.
Then we will discuss our affairs."

Zap 210 stood paralyzed by indecision. She tentatively tried to shrink away from the man's grasp, which

only tightened. Zap 210 winced. "Come," said the man. She stumbled with him to a nearby booth.

The man signaled; a jug of white wine and a platter of fried fishcakes was set before them. "Eat," the man told her. "Drink. I stint no one, either in bounty or hard knocks." He poured her a liberal goblet of wine. "Now, before we proceed, what are your fees? Certain of your number, knowing me for Otwile, have attempted nothing less than larceny—to their dissatisfaction, I may say. So then: your price?"

"Price for what?" whispered Zap 210.

Otwile's blue eyes widened in surprise. "You are an odd one. What is your race? You are too pale for a Thang, too slender for a Gray."

Zap 210 lowered her eyes. She tasted the wine, then searched desperately over her shoulder for Reith.

"Ah, but you are shy!" declared Otwile. "And delicate of manner as well!"

He began to eat. Zap 210 tried to slip away. "Sit!" snapped Otwile. She hastily returned to her seat. "Drink!" She sipped at the wine, which was stronger than any she had yet tasted.

"That is better," said Otwile. "Now we understand each other."

"No," said Zap 210 in her soft voice. "We don't! I don't want to be here! What do you want of me?"

Otwile again stared at her in disbelief. "You don't know?"

"Of course not. Unless—you don't mean *that?*"

Otwile grinned. "I mean precisely that, and more."

"But—I don't know anything about such things! I don't want to learn."

Otwile put down his fishcakes. He said incredulously, "A virgin, wearing a sash. Is that how you represent yourself?"

"I don't know what such a thing is. . . . I must go, to find Adam Reith."

"You have found me, which is somewhat better. Drink wine, to relax yourself. Today is to be that particular day you will remember to the end of your time." Otwile poured full the goblets. "Indeed, I will join you, to relax myself. Truth to tell, I myself have become somewhat excited!"

Reith and Cauch walked through the bazaar, where the fish and produce vendors called attention to their merchandise by means of peculiar ululations.

"Are they singing?" asked Reith.

"No," said Cauch, the cries were no more than devices to attract attention. "The Thang have no great feeling for music. The selling-screams of the fish-wives are inventive and emotional, true; listen and you will hear how they try to outdo each other!"

Reith conceded that certain of the advertisements were remarkably intricate. "In due course the social anthropologists will record and codify these calls. But for the moment I am more interested in the eel-races."

"To be sure," said Cauch. "Though, as you will notice, they are not yet in operation."

They crossed the compound and stood appraising the vacant tables, the reservoir and the chute. Looking across the wall, Reith noticed the fronds of a gnarled old psilla. "I want to look on the other side of the wall," he said.

"Just so," said Cauch, "and I have the fullest sympathy with your curiosity. But are we not at the moment directing our energies to the eel-races?"

"We are," said Reith. "I see a portal through the wall, opposite that vendor of amulets. Do you care to accompany me?"

"Certainly," said Cauch. "I am always alert to learn."

They walked along beside the old wall, which in the remote past had been faced with brown and white tiles, most of which had fallen away, revealing patches of dark brown brick. Passing through the portal, they entered Urmank Old Town: a district of huts built of broken tile, brick, fragments of stone, and odd lengths of timber. Some were abandoned ruins, others were in the process of construction: a continuing cycle of decay and regeneration, in which every shard, every stick, every fragment of stone had been used a hundred times over twice as many generations. Low-caste Thangs and a squat, big-headed variety of Gray peered forth from the doorways as Reith and Cauch went past; stench thickened the air.

Beyond the huts lay an area of rubble, puddles of slime, a few clumps of angry red bristle-bush. Reith located the psilla of which he had taken note: it stood close beside the wall, overhanging a shed built of well-laid bricks. The door was solid timber bound with iron, secured with a heavy iron lock. The shed backed firmly up against the wall.

Reith looked around the landscape, which was vacant except for a group of naked children paddling in a rivulet of yellow slime. He approached the shed. The lock, the hasp, the hinges were sound and solid. There was no window to the shed, nor any opening other than the door. Reith backed away. "We've seen all we need to see."

"Indeed?" Cauch dubiously inspected the shed, the wall, the psilla tree. "I see nothing significant. Are you still referring to the eel-races?"

"Of course." They went back through the dismal huddle of huts. Reith said: "Very likely we could make all our arrangements alone; still, the help of two trustworthy men might prove convenient."

Cauch eyed him with awe and incredulity. "You seriously hope to take money from the eel-race?"

"If the eel-master pays all winning bets, I do."

"No fear of that," said Cauch. "He will pay, assuming that there are winnings. And on this supposition, how do you propose to share?"

"Half for me, half for you and your two men."

Cauch pursed his lips. "I perceive something of an inequity. From a mutual project, one man should not derive three times the share of the others."

"I believe that he should," said Reith, "when otherwise the other three gain nothing whatever."

"The point is well-taken," Cauch admitted. "The affair shall go as you recommend."

They returned to the café. Reith looked for Zap 210, who was nowhere to be seen. "I must find my companion," he told Cauch. "No doubt she waits at the inn."

Cauch made an affable gesture; Reith went to the inn, but found Zap 210 nowhere. Making inquiries of the clerk he learned that she had come and gone, leaving no intimation as to her destination.

Reith went to the doorway and looked up and down the quay. To the right porters in faded red kirtles and leather shoulderpads unloaded a cog; to the left was the bustle of the bazaar.

He never should have left her alone, he told himself, especially in her mood of the morning. He had taken her stability for granted, never troubling to divine the state of her mind. Reith cursed himself for callousness and egocentricity. The girl had been undergoing the most intense and dramatic emotional strains: all the fundamental processes of life at once. Reith strode back to the café. Cauch eyed him with calm benevolence. "You appear concerned."

"The girl who accompanies me—I can't find her."

"Pah," said Cauch. "They are all alike. She has gone to the bazaar, to buy a trinket."

"No. She has no money. She is utterly inexperienced; she would go nowhere—except . . ." Reith turned to look toward the hills, the way to which lay between the ghoul-castles. Would she seriously consider going down into the Shelters? . . . A new idea came to turn his bones to ice. The Gzhindra. Reith summoned the Thang servant-boy. "I breakfasted this morning with a young woman. Do you recall her?"

"Yes, indeed; she wore an orange turban, like a Hedaijhan, at least on that occasion."

"You saw her another time?"

"I did. She sat yonder, wearing the sash of solicitation and consorting with Otwile the champion. They drank wine for a period, then went off."

"She went of her own free will?" asked Reith in wonder.

The servant gave a shrug of indifference, covertly insolent. "She wore the sash, she uttered no outcry, she leaned on his arm, perhaps to steady herself, for I believe her to have been somewhat drunk."

"Where did they go?"

Again the shrug. "Otwile's chambers are not too far distant; perhaps this was their resort."

"Show me the way."

"No no." The servant shook his head. "I am at my duties. Also I would not care to vex Otwile."

Reith jumped at him; the servant stumbled back in a panic. "Quick!" hissed Reith.

"This way then, but hurry; I am not supposed to leave the café."

They ran through the dank back alleys of Urmank, in and out of the brown light of Carina 4269, which occasionally slanted down past the crooked gables of the tall houses. The servant halted, pointed along a walkway leading into a garden of green and purple foliage. "At the back of the shrubbery are Otwile's rooms." He scuttled back the way he had come. Reith ran along the walkway, through the garden. At the back stood a cottage of carved timber and panels of translucent fiber. As Reith approached he heard a sudden wordless cry of outrage from within. "Unclean!" Then there was the sound of a blow, and a whimper. Reith's knees shook, he tottered forward, thrust open the door. On the floor crouched Zap 210, glassy-eyed and nude; above her stood Otwile. Zap 210 stared at Reith; he saw a red welt on her cheek.

Otwile spoke in a voice of hushed outrage. "Who are you to intrude in my house?"

Reith ignored him. He picked up Zap 210's undergown, a torn tangle of cloth. He turned to look at Otwile. Cauch spoke from the doorway. "Come, Adam Reith; fetch the girl. Do not trouble yourself."

Reith paid no heed. He moved slowly toward Otwile, who waited, smiling coldly, hands on hips. Reith approached to within three feet. Otwile, six inches taller, smiled down at him.

Zap 210 said in a husky croak: "It wasn't his fault. I wore an orange sash . . . I didn't know . . ."

Reith turned slowly away. He found Zap 210's gray gown, pulled it over her slender body. He saw what had outraged Otwile; he could hardly control a great cry to express sorrow and pity and terrible grim amusement. He put his arm around Zap 210 and started to lead her from the room.

Otwile was dissatisfied. He had been awaiting a touch, a motion, even a word, to serve as a trigger for his muscles. Was he to be denied even the gratification of beating the man who had invaded his chambers? The bubble of his rage burst. He bounced forward and swung his leg in a kick.

Reith was pleased to find Otwile active. Twisting, he caught Otwile's ankle, pulled, dragged the champion hoping out into the garden, and sent him careening into a thicket of scarlet bamboo. Otwile sprang forth like a leopard. He halted, stood with arms out, grimacing hideously, clenching and unclenching his hands. Reith punched him in the face. Otwile seemed not to notice. He reached for Reith, who backed away, hacking at the heavy wrists. Otwile came forward, crowding Reith against the side-wall. Reith feinted, punched with his left hand and rapped his knuckles into Otwile's face. Otwile gave a small flat-footed jump forward, and another, then he gave a hideous rasping scream, and swung his great arm in an open-handed slap. Reith ducked below, hit Otwile full in the belly, and as Otwile jerked up his knee, seized the crooked leg, heaved up, and sent Otwile down flat on his back with a thud like a falling tree. For a moment Otwile lay dazed, then he slowly struggled to a sitting position. With a single backward glance Reith led Zap 210 from the garden. Cauch bowed politely toward Otwile and followed.

Reith took Zap 210 to the inn. She sat on the couch in her cubicle, clutching the gray gown about herself, limp and miserable. Reith sat down beside her. "What happened?"

Tears dripped down her cheeks; she held her hands to her face. Reith stroked her head. Presently she wiped her eyes. "I don't know what I did wrong—unless it was the sash. He made me drink wine until I became dizzy. He took me through the streets . . . I felt very strange. I could hardly walk. In the house I wouldn't take off my clothes and he became angry. Then he saw me and he became even angrier. He said I was unclean. . . . I don't know what to do with myself. I'm sick, I'm dying."

Reith said, "No, you're not sick or dying. Your body has started to function normally. There's nothing whatever wrong with you."

"I'm not unclean?"

"Of course not." Reith rose to his feet. "I'll send in a maid to take care of you. Then just lie quietly and sleep until I return—I hope with enough money to put us aboard a ship."

Zap 210 nodded listlessly; Reith departed the cubicle.

At the café Reith found Cauch and two young Zsafathrans who had come to Urmank aboard the second cart. "This is Schazar; this is Widisch," said Cauch. "Both are reckoned competent; I have no doubt but that they will fulfill any reasonable requirements."

"In that case," said Reith, "let's be off about our business. We haven't too much time to spare, or so I should judge."

The four sauntered off down the quay. Reith explained his theories: "—which now we must put to the test. Mind you, I may be wrong, in which case the project will fail."

"No," said Cauch. "You have employed an extraordinary mental process to adduce what I now see to be limpid truth."

"The process is called logic," said Reith. "It is not always dependable. But we shall see."

They passed the eel-race table, where a few folk had already settled at the benches, ready for the day's gambling. Reith hurried his steps: under the portal, through the dismal byways of Urmank Old Town, toward the shed under the psilla tree. They halted fifty yards away and took cover in a ruined hut at the edge of the wastelands.

Ten minutes passed. Reith began to fidget. "I can't believe that we've come too late."

The young man Schazar pointed across the wastes, to the far end of the wall. "Two men."

The men strolled closer. One affected the flowing white robes and square white hat of an Erze Island Sage: "The eel-master," muttered Cauch. The other, a young man, wore a pink skullcap and a light pink cape. The two walked casually and confidently along the trail and parted company near the shed. The eel-master continued toward the portal. Widisch said: "Easier merely to waylay the old charlatan and divest him of his pouch; the effect, after all, is the same."

"Unfortunately," said Cauch, "he carries no sequins on his person, and makes the fact well known. His funds are brought to the eel-races daily by four armed slaves under the supervision of his chief wife."

The young man in pink strolled to the shed. He fitted a key in the lock, turned it three times, opened the ponderous door and entered the shed. He turned with surprise to find that Reith and Schazar had also pushed into the shed beside him. He attempted to bluster. "What is the meaning of this?"

"I will speak one time only," said Reith. "We want your unstinting cooperation; otherwise we will hang you by the toes to yonder psilla. Is this clear?"

"I understand perfectly," said the young man with a quaver.

"Describe the routine."

The young man hesitated. Reith nodded to Schazar, who brought forth a coil of hard cord. The young man said quickly, "The routine is quite simple. I undress and step into the tank." He indicated a cylindrical pool four feet in diameter at the back of the shed. "A tube communicates with the reservoir; the level in the tank and that in the reservoir are the same. I swim through the tube to the reservoir and come up into a space in the peripheral frame. As soon as the lid is lowered, I open a partition. I reach into the reservoir and move the specified eel to the edge of the chute."

"And how is the color specified?"

"By the eel-master's finger-taps on the top of the lid."

Reith turned to Cauch. "Schazar and I are now in control. I suggest that you now take your places at the table." He spoke to the young man in pink: "Is there sufficient space for two under the reservoir?"

"Yes," said the young man grudgingly. "Just barely. But tell me: if I cooperate with you, how will I protect myself from the eel-master?"

"Be frank with him," said Reith. "State that you value your life more than his sequins."

"He will say that as far as he is concerned, affairs are reversed."

"Too bad," said Reith. "The hazard of your trade. How soon should we be in position?"

"Within a minute or so."

Reith removed his outer garments. "If by some ineptness we are detected . . . surely the consequences are as plain to you as to me."

The apprentice merely grunted. He doffed his pink robe. "Follow me." He stepped into the tank. "The way is dark but straight."

Reith joined him in the tank. The young man drew a deep breath and submerged; Reith did the same. At the bottom, finding a horizontal tube about three feet in diameter, he pulled himself through, staying close behind the apprentice.

They surfaced in a space about four feet long, a foot

and a half high, a foot wide. Light entered through artfully arranged crevices, which also allowed a view over
the gaming tables; Reith thus could see that both
Cauch and Widisch had found places along the
counter.

From near at hand came the eel-master's voice.
"Welcome all to another day of exciting races. Who
will win? Who will lose? No one knows. It may be me,
it may be you. But we all will enjoy the fun of the
races. For those who are new to our little game, you
will notice that the board before you is marked with
eleven colors. You may bet any amount on any of the
colors. If your color wins, you are paid ten times the
amount of your bet. Note these eels and their colors:
white, gray, tawny, light blue, brown, dark red, vermilion, blue, green, violet, black. Are there any questions?"

"Yes," called Cauch. "Is there any limit on the betting?"

"The case now being delivered contains ten thousand sequins. This is my limit; I pay no more. Please
place your bets."

With a practiced eye the eel-master appraised the
table. He lifted the lid, set the eels into the center of
the reservoir. "No more betting, please." On the lid
sounded *tap-tap tap-tap*.

"Two-two," whispered the apprentice. "That's
green." He pushed aside a panel and reaching into the
reservoir, seized the green eel and set it into the mouth
of the chute. Then he drew back and closed the panel.

"Green wins!" called the eel-master. "So then—I
pay! Twenty sequins to this sturdy seafarer. . . . Make
your bets, please."

Tap tap-tap-tap sounded on the lid. "Vermilion,"
whispered the apprentice. He performed as before.

"Vermilion wins!" called the eel-master.

Reith kept his eye to the crack. On each occasion
Cauch and Widisch had risked a pair of sequins. On
the third betting round each placed thirty sequins on
white.

"Bets are now made," came the eel-master's voice. The lid came down. *Tap tap* came the sounds.

"Brown," whispered the apprentice.

"White," said Reith. "The white eel wins."

The apprentice groaned in muted distress. He put the white eel into the chute.

"Another contest between these baffling little creatures," came the complacent voice of the eel-master. "On this occasion the winning color is—brown. . . . Brown? White. Yes, white it is! Ha! In my old age I become color-blind. Tribulation for a poor old man! . . . A pair of handsome winners here! Three hundred sequins for you, three hundred sequins for you. . . . Take your winnings, gentlemen. What? You are betting the entire sum, both of you?"

"Yes, luck appears to be with us today."

"Both on dark red?"

"Yes; notice the flight of yonder blood-birds! This is a portent."

The eel-master smiled off into the sky. "Who can divine the ways of nature? I pray that you are incorrect. Well, then, all bets are made? Then in with the eels, down with the lid, and let the most determined eel issue forth the winner." His hand rested a moment on the lid; his fingernail struck the surface a single time. "They twist, they search, the light beckons; we should soon have a winner. . . . Here comes—is it blue?" He gave an involuntary groan. "Dark red." He peered into the faces of the Zsafathrans. "Your presages, astonishingly, were correct."

"Yes," said Cauch. "Did I not tell you as much? Pay over our winnings."

Slowly the eel-master counted out three thousand-worth of sequins to each. "Astonishing." He glanced thoughtfully toward the reservoir. "Do you observe any further portents?"

"Nothing significant. But I will bet nonetheless. A hundred sequins on black."

"I bet the same," declared Widisch.

The eel-master hesitated. He rubbed his chin, looked

around the counter. "Extraordinary." He put the eels into the reservoir. "Are all bets laid?" His hand rested on the lid; as if by nervous mannerism he brought his fingernails down in two sharp raps. "Very well; I open the gate." He pulled the lever and strode up to the end of the chute. "And here comes—what color? Black!"

"Excellent!" declared Cauch. "We reap a return after years of squandering money upon your perverse eels! Pay over our gains, if you please!"

"Certainly," croaked the eel-master. "But I can work no more. I suffer from an aching of the joints; the eel-racing is at an end."

Reith and the apprentice immediately returned to the shed. The apprentice donned his pink cape and hat and took to his heels.

Reith and Schazar returned through the Old Town to the portal, where they encountered the eel-master, who strode past in a great flapping of his white gown. The normally benign face was mottled red; he carried a stout stave, which he swung in short ominous jerks.

Cauch and Widisch awaited them on the quay. Cauch handed Reith a pleasantly plump pouch. "Your share of the winnings: four thousand sequins. The day has been edifying."

"We have done well," said Reith. "Our association has been mutually helpful, which is a rare thing for Tschai!"

"For our part we return instantly to Zsafathra," said Cauch. "What of you?"

"Urgent business calls me onward. Like yourselves, my companion and I depart as soon as possible."

"In that case, farewell." The three Zsafathrans went their way. Reith turned into the bazaar, where he made a variety of purchases. Back at the hotel he went to Zap 210's cubicle and rapped at the door, his heart pounding with anticipation.

"Who is it?" came a soft voice.

"It is I, Adam Reith."

"A moment." The door opened. Zap 210 stood fac-

ing him, face flushed and drowsy. She wore the gray
smock which she had only just pulled over her head.

Reith took his bundles to the couch. "This—and
this—and this—and this—for you."

"For me? What are they?"

"Look and see."

With a diffident side-glance toward Reith, she
opened the bundles, then for a period stood looking
down at the articles they contained.

Reith asked uneasily, "Do you like them?"

She turned to him a hurt gaze. "Is this how you
want me to be—like the others?"

Reith stood nonplussed. It was not the reaction he
had expected. He said carefully, "We will be traveling.
It is best that we go as inconspicuously as possible.
Remember the Gzhindra? We must dress like the folk
we travel among."

"I see."

"Which do you like best?"

Zap 210 lifted the dark green gown, laid it down,
took up the blood-orange smock and dull white pantaloons, then the rather jaunty light brown suit with the
black vest and short black cape. "I don't know whether
I like any of them."

"Try one on."

"Now?"

"Certainly!"

Zap 210 held up first one of the garments, then another. She looked at Reith; he grinned. "Very well, I'll
go."

In his own cubicle he changed into the fresh garments he had bought for himself: gray breeches, a
dark-blue jacket. The gray furze smock he decided to
discard. As he threw it aside he felt the outline of the
portfolio, which after a moment's hesitation he transferred to the inner lining of his new jacket. Such a set
of documents, if for no other reason, had value as a
curio. He went to the common room. Presently Zap
210 appeared. She wore the dark green gown. "Why
do you stare at me?" she asked.

Reith could not tell her the truth, that he was recalling the first time he had seen her: a neurasthenic waif shrouded in a black cloak, pallid and bone-thin. She retained something of her dreaming wistful look, but her pallor had become a smooth sun-shadowed ivory; her black hair curled in ringlets over her forehead and ears.

"I was thinking," said Reith, "that the gown suits you very well."

She made a faint grimace: a twitch of the lips approaching a smile.

They walked out upon the quay, to the cog *Nhiahar*. They found the taciturn master in the saloon, working over his accounts. "You desire passage to Kazain? There is only the grand cabin to be had at seven hundred sequins, or I can give you two berths in the dormitory, at two hundred."

Chapter 9

A dead calm held the Second Sea. The *Nhiahar* slid out of the inlet, propelled by its field engine; by degrees Urmank faded into the murk of distance.

The *Nhiahar* moved in silence except for the gurgle of water under the bow. The only other passengers were a pair of waxen-faced old women swathed in gray gauze who appeared briefly on deck, then crept to their dark little cabin.

Reith was well-satisfied with the grand cabin. It ranged the entire width of the ship, with three great windows overlooking the sea astern. In alcoves to port and starboard were well-cushioned beds, as soft as any Reith had felt on Tschai, if a trifle musty. In the center stood a massive table of carved black wood, with a pair of equally massive chairs at either end. Zap 210 made a sulky appraisal of the room. Today she wore the dull white trousers with the orange blouse; she seemed keyed up and tense, and moved with nervous abruptness in jerks and halts and fidgeting twitches of the fingers.

Reith watched her covertly, trying to calculate the exact nature of her mood. She refused to look toward him or meet his gaze. At last he asked: "Do you like the ship?"

She gave a sullen shrug. "I have never seen anything like it before." She went to the door, where she turned him a sour twitch of a smile—a derisive grimace—and went out on deck.

Reith looked up at the overhead, shrugged, and after a final glance around the room, followed her.

She had climbed the companionway to the quarter-deck, where she stood leaning on the taff-rail, looking back the way they had come. Reith seated himself on a bench nearby and pretended to bask in the wan brown sunlight while he puzzled over her behavior. She was female and inherently irrational—but her conduct seemed to exceed this elemental fact. Certain of her attitudes had been formed in the Shelters, but these seemed to be waning; upon reaching the surface she had abandoned the old life and discarded its point of view, as an insect molts a skin. In the process, Reith ruminated, she had discarded her old personality—but had not yet discovered a new one. . . . The thought gave Reith a qualm. Part of the girl's charm or fascination, or whatever it was, lay in her innocence, her transparency . . . transparency? Reith made a skeptical sound. Not altogether. He went to join her. "What are you pondering so deeply?"

She gave him a cool side-glance. "I was thinking of myself and the wide *ghaun*. I remembered my time in the dark. I know now that below the world I was not yet born. All those years, while I moved quietly below, the folk of the surface lived in color and change and air."

"So this is why you've been acting so strangely!"

"No!" she cried in sudden passion. "It is not! The reason is you and your secrecy! You tell me nothing. I don't know where we are going, or what you are going to do with me."

Reith frowned down at the black boil of the wake. "I'm not sure of these things myself."

"But you must know something!"

"Yes. . . . When I get to Sivishe I want to return to my home, which is far and remote."

"And what of me?"

And what of Zap 210? wondered Reith. A question he had avoided asking himself. "I'm not sure you'd want to come with me," he replied, somewhat lamely.

Tears glinted in her eyes. "Where else can I go?

Should I become a drudge? Or a Gzhindra? Or wear an orange sash at Urmank? Or should I die?" She swung away and marched forward to the bow, past a group of the spade-faced seamen, who watched her from the side of their pale eyes.

Reith returned to the bench. . . . The afternoon passed. Black clouds to the north generated a cool wind. The sails were shaken out, and the cog drove forward. Zap 210 presently came aft with a strange expression on her face. She gave Reith a look of sad accusation and went down to the cabin.

Reith followed and found her laying on one of the couches. "Don't you feel well?"

"No."

"Come outside. You'll be worse in here."

She staggered out upon the deck.

"Keep your eyes on the horizon," said Reith. "When the ship moves, keep your head level. Do that for a while and you'll feel better."

Zap 210 stood by the rail. The clouds loomed overhead and the wind died; the *Nhiahar* lay wallowing with slatting sails. . . . From the sky came a purple dazzle, slanting and slashing at the sea—once, twice, three times, all in the flicker of an eye-blink. Zap 210 gave a small scream and jerked back in terror. Reith caught her and held her as the thunder rumbled down. She moved uneasily; Reith kissed her forehead, her face, her mouth.

The sun settled into a tattered panoply of gold and black and brown; with the dusk came rain. Reith and Zap 210 retreated to their cabin, where the steward served supper: mincemeat, sea-fruit, biscuits. They ate, looking out through the great windows at the sea and rain and lightning, and afterwards, with lightning sparking the dark, they became lovers.

At midnight the clouds departed; stars burnt down from the sky. "Look up there!" said Reith. "Among the stars are other worlds of men. One of them is called Earth." He paused. Zap 210 lay listening, but

Reith for some obscure reason could say no more, and presently she fell asleep.

The *Nhiahar*, driven by fair winds, plunged down the Second Sea, crashing through great white billows of foam. Cape Braise reared up ahead; the ship put into the ancient stone city Stheine to take on water, then fared forth into the Schanizade.

Twenty miles down the coast a tongue of land hooked out to the west. Along the foreshore a forest of dark blue trees shrouded a city of flat domes, cambered cusps, sweeping colonnades. Reith thought to recognize the architecture, and put a question to the captain: "Is that a Chasch city?"

"It is Songh, most southerly of the Blue Chasch places. I have taken cargoes into Songh, but it is risky business. You must know the games of the Chasch: antics of a dying race. I have seen ruins on the Kotan steppes: a hundred places where Old Chasch or Blue Chasch once lived, and who goes there now? Only the Phung."

The city receded into the distance and disappeared from view as the ship passed south beyond the peninsula. Not long after a cry from one of the crew brought everyone out on deck. In the sky a pair of airships fought. One was a gleaming contrivance of blue and white metal, shaped to a set of splendid curves. A balustrade contained the deck, on which lay a dozen creatures in glistening casques. The other craft was austere and bleak: a vessel sinister, ugly, gray, built with only its function in mind. It was slightly smaller than the Blue Chasch ship and somewhat more agile; in the dorsal bubble crouched the Dirdir crew, intent at the work of destroying the Chasch ship. The vessels circled and swung, now high, now low, careening around each other like venomous insects. From time to time, as circumstances offered, the ships exchanged volleys of sand-blast fire, without noticeable effect. Far up into the gray-brown sky spun the sparkling shapes, to spiral giddily down, one after the other, veering only yards above the ocean's surface.

The whole company of the *Nhiahar* came on deck to watch the battle, even the two old women who had not previously shown themselves. As they scanned the sky the hood fell back from the head of one of them, to reveal a keen pale countenance. Zap 210, standing beside Reith, uttered a soft gasp, and quickly turned away her gaze.

The Blue Chasch ship slid suddenly down; the bow guns struck under the counter of the Dirdir ship, knocking it up, tumbling it over and down into the sea, where it struck with a soundless splash. The Blue Chasch vessel swung in a single grand circle, then cruised back toward Songh.

The old women had disappeared below. Zap 210 spoke in a tremulous whisper: "Did you notice?"

"Yes. I noticed."

"They are Gzhindra."

"Are you sure?"

"Yes, I am sure."

"I suppose Gzhindra make voyages like other folk," said Reith, somewhat hollowly. "So far at least they've done nothing to bother us."

"But they are here, aboard the ship! They do nothing without purpose!"

Reith made another skeptical sound. "Perhaps so— but what can we do about it?"

"We can kill them!"

Zap 210, for all the strictures of her upbringing, was still a creature of Tschai, thought Reith. He said: "We'll keep close watch on them. Now that we know who they are, and they don't know that we know, the advantage is ours."

It was Zap 210's turn to make a skeptical sound. Reith nevertheless refused to waylay the old women in the dark and strangle them.

The voyage proceeded, southwest toward the Saschan Islands. Days passed without event more noteworthy than the turn of the heavens. Each morning

Carina 4269 broke through the horizon into a dull bronze and old rose dawn. By noon a high haze had formed, to filter the sunlight and lay a sheen like antique silk on the water. The afternoons were long; sunsets were sad glories: allegorical wars between dark heroes and the lords of light. After nightfall the moons appeared: sometimes pink Az, sometimes blue Braz, and sometimes the *Nhiahar* rode alone under the stars.

For Reith the days and nights would have been as pleasant as any he had known on Tschai except for the worry which nagged him: what was happening at Sivishe? Would he find the space-boat intact or destroyed? What of crafty Aila Woudiver; what of the Dirdir in their horrid city across the water? And what of the two old women, who might be Gzhindra? They never appeared except in the deep of night, to walk the foredeck. One dark evening Reith watched them, the hair prickling at the nape of his neck. Either they were Gzhindra or they were not, but lacking information Reith felt obliged to assume the worst—and the implications were cause for the most dismal foreboding.

One pale umber morning the Saschan Islands loomed out of the sea: three ancient volcanic necks surrounded by shelves of detritus where grew groves of psilla, kianthus, candlenut, lethipod. On each island a town climbed the central crag, beehive huts stacked one on the other like the cells of a wasp-nest. Black openings stared out to sea; wisps of smoke rose into the air.

The *Nhiahar* entered the inner bay and, swerving to avoid a ferry, approached the south island. On the dock waited bowlegged Saschanese longshoremen in black breech-clouts and black roll-toed ankle-boots. They took the hawsers; the *Nhiahar* was warped alongside. As soon as the gangplank settled into place the longshoremen swarmed aboard. Hatches were opened; bales of leather, sacks of pilgrim-pod meal, crated tools were taken to the dock.

Reith and Zap 210 went ashore. The captain called dourly after them: "I make departure at noon exactly, aboard or not."

The two walked along the esplanade, the crag and its unnatural incrustation of huts rearing above them. Zap 210 glanced over her shoulder. "They are following us."

"The Gzhindra?"

"Yes."

Reith grunted in disgust. "It's definite then. They have orders not to let us out of their sight."

"And we are as good as dead." Zap 210 spoke in a colorless voice. "At Kazain they will report to the Pnume and then nothing can help us; we'll be taken down into the dark."

Reith could think of nothing to say. They came to a small harbor protected from the sea by a pair of jetties, which narrowed to become a ferry slip. Reith and Zap 210 paused to watch the ferry arrive from the outer islands: a wide scow with control cabins at either end, carrying two hundred Saschanese of all ages and qualities. It nosed into the slip; the passengers debarked. As many more paid toll to a fat man sitting before a booth and surged aboard; immediately the ferry departed. Reith watched it cross the water, then led Zap 210 to a waiting area set with benches and tables beside the ferry slip. Reith ordered sweet wine and biscuits from a serving boy, then went to confer with the fat fare-collector. Zap 210 looked nervously here and there. In the shadow of a flight of steps she thought to glimpse two shapes robed in gray. *They wonder what we're doing,* Zap 210 told herself.

Reith returned. "The next ferry leaves in something over an hour—a few minutes before noon. I've already paid our fares."

Zap 210 gave him a puzzled inspection. "But we must be aboard the *Nhiahar* at noon!"

"True. Are the Gzhindra nearby?"

"They've just taken seats at the far table."

Reith managed a grim chuckle. "We're giving them something to think about."

"What should they think about? That we might take the ferry?"

"Something of the sort."

"But why should they think that? It seems so strange!"

"Not altogether. There might be a ship at one of the other islands to take us somewhere beyond their knowledge."

"Is there such a ship?"

"None that I know of."

"But if we take the ferry the Gzhindra will follow, and the *Nhiahar* will leave without all of us!"

"I expect so. The captain would have no qualms whatever."

The minutes passed. Zap 210 began to fidget. "Noon is very close." She studied Reith, wondering what went on in his mind. No other man of Tschai—at least none she had yet seen—resembled him; he was a different sort.

"Here comes the ferry," said Reith. "Let's go down to the slip. We want to be the first in line."

Zap 210 rose to her feet. Never would she understand Reith! She followed him down to the waiting area. Others came to join them, to push and squirm and mutter. Reith asked: "What of the Gzhindra?"

Zap 210 glanced over her shoulder. "They're standing at the back of the crowd."

The ferry entered the slip; the barriers opened and the passengers surged ashore.

Reith spoke in Zap 210's ear. "Walk close by the collector's hut. As we pass, duck inside."

"Oh."

The gate opened. Reith and Zap 210 half-walked, half-ran down the way. At the collector's hut, Reith lowered his head and slipped within; Zap 210 followed. The embarking passengers, pushing past, handed their fares to the collector and marched down to the ferry. Near the end of the line came the Gzhindra, trying to peer through the surge ahead of them. They moved with the crowd, down the ramp, aboard the ferry.

The barrier closed; the ferry moved out. Reith and Zap 210 emerged from the hut. "It's almost noon," said Reith. "Time to return aboard the *Nhiahar*."

Chapter 10

Southeast toward Kislovan gusty winds drove the *Nhiahar*. The sea was almost black. The swells which rolled up and under the ship spilled rushes of white foam ahead.

One blustery morning Zap 210 joined Reith where he stood at the bow. For a moment they stood looking ahead across the heaving water to where Carina 4269 dropped prisms and fractured shards of golden light.

Zap 210 asked, "What lies ahead?"

Reith shook his head. "I don't know. I wish I did."

"But you worry. Are you afraid?"

"I'm afraid of a man named Aila Woudiver. I don't know whether he's alive or dead."

"Who is Aila Woudiver, that you fear him so?"

"A man of Sivishe, a man to fear. . . . I think he must be dead. I was kidnapped out of a dream. In the dream I saw Aila Woudiver's head split open."

"So why do you worry?"

Sooner or later, thought Reith, he must make all clear. Perhaps now was the time. "Remember the night I told you of other worlds among the stars?"

"I remember."

"One of these worlds is Earth. At Sivishe I built a spaceship, with Aila Woudiver's help. I want to go to Earth."

Zap 210 stared ahead across the water. "Why do you want to go to Earth?"

"I was born there. It is my home."

"Oh." She spoke in a colorless voice. After a reflective silence of fifteen seconds, she turned him a side-long glance.

Reith said ruefully, "You wonder if I am insane."

"I've wondered many times. Many, many times."

Though Reith himself had put the suggestion, he was nonetheless taken aback. "Indeed?"

She smiled her sad grimace of a smile. "Consider what you have done. In the Shelters. At the Khor grove. When you changed eels at Urmank."

"Acts of desperation, acts of a frantic Earthman."

Zap 210 brooded across the windy ocean. "If you are an Earthman, what do you do here on Tschai?"

"On the Kotan steppes my spaceship was wrecked. At Sivishe I've built another."

"Hmmf. . . . Is Earth such a paradise?"

"The people of Earth know nothing of Tschai. It's important that they do know."

"Why?"

"A dozen reasons. Most important, the Dirdir raided Earth once; they might decide to return."

She gave him her swift side-glance. "You have friends on Earth?"

"Of course."

"You lived there in a house?"

"In a manner of speaking."

"With a woman? And your children?"

"No woman, no children. I've been a spaceman all my life."

"And when you return—what then?"

"I'm not thinking past Sivishe right now."

"You will take me with you?"

Reith put his arm around her. "Yes. I will take you with me."

She heaved a sigh of relief. Presently she pointed ahead. "Beyond where the sun glints—an island."

The island, a great crag of barren black basalt, was the first of a myriad, to scarify the surface of the sea. The area was home to a host of sea-foragers, of a sort beyond Reith's previous experience. Four oscillating wings supported a cluster of dangling pink tentacles and a central tube ending in a bulbous eye. The creatures drifted high and low, dipping suddenly to seize some small wriggling sea-thing. A few drifted toward the *Nhiahar*; the crewmen lurched back in dread and took shelter in the forecastle.

The captain, who had come up on the foredeck, sneered in disgust. "They consider these the guts and eyes of drowned seamen. We sail the Channel of Death; these rocks are the Charnel Teeth."

"How do you navigate by night?"

"I don't know," said the captain, "for I have never tried. It is risky enough by day. Around each of those rocks lies a hundred hulks and heaped white bones. Do you notice, far ahead, the loom? There is Kislovan! Tomorrow will find us docked at Kazain."

As evening approached long strands of clouds raced across the sky and the wind began to moan. The captain took the *Nhiahar* into the lee of one of the larger black rocks, nosing close, close, close, until the sprit almost scraped the wet black stone. Here the anchor was dropped and the *Nhiahar* rode in relative safety as the wind became a screaming gale. Great swells drove through the black crags; foam crashed high up and fell slowly back. The sea boiled and surged; the *Nhiahar* wallowed, jerking at the anchor line, then floating suddenly loose and free.

With the coming of darkness the wind died. For a long period the sea rose and fell in fretful recollection, but dawn found the Charnel Teeth standing like archaic monuments on a sea of brown glass. Beyond lay the bulk of the continent.

Proceeding through the Charnel Teeth under power, the *Nhiahar* at noon nosed into a long narrow bay and by late afternoon drew alongside the pier at Kazain.

On the dock two Dirdirmen paused to watch the *Nhiahar*. Their caste was high, perhaps Immaculate; they were young and vain; they wore their false effulgences aslant and glittering. Reith's heart rose in his throat for fear that they had been sent to take him into custody. For such a contingency he had no plans; he sweated until the two sauntered off toward the Dirdir settlement at the head of the bay.

There were no formalities at the dock; Reith and Zap 210 carried their belongings ashore and without interference made their way to the motor-wagon depot. An eight-wheeled vehicle stood on the verge of departure across the neck of Kislovan; Reith commissioned the most luxurious accommodation available: a cubicle of two hammocks on the third tier with access to the rear deck.

An hour later the motor-wagon trundled forth from Kazain. For a space the road climbed into the coastal uplands, affording a view over the Channel of Death and the Charnel Teeth. Five miles north the road swung inland. For the rest of the day the motor-wagon lumbered beside bean-vine fields, forests of white ghost-apple, an occasional little village.

In the early evening the motor-wagon halted at an isolated inn, where the forty-three passengers took supper. About half seemed to be Grays; the rest were people Reith could not identify. A pair might have been steppe-men of Kotan; several conceivably were Saschanese. Two yellow-skinned women in gowns of black scales almost certainly were Marsh-folk from the north shore of the Second Sea. The various groups took the least possible notice of each other, eating and returning at once to board the power-wagon. The indifference Reith knew to be feigned; each had gauged the exact quality of all the others with a precision beyond any Reith could muster.

Early in the morning the power-wagon once more set forth and met the dawn climbing over the edge of the central plateau. Carina 4269 rose to illuminate a vast savanna, clumped with alumes, gallow-trees, bundle-fungus, patches of thorn-grass.

So passed the day, and four more: a journey which Reith hardly noticed for his mounting tension. In the Shelters, on the great subterranean canal, along the shores of the Second Sea, at Urmank, even aboard the *Nhiahar*, he had been calm with the patience of despair. The stakes were once again high. He hoped, he dreaded, he strained for the power-wagon to go faster, he shrank from the thought of what he might find in the warehouse on the Sivishe salt flats. Zap 210, reacting to Reith's tension, or perhaps beset with premonitions of her own, retired into herself, and took small interest in the passing landscape.

Over the central plateau, down through a badlands of eroded granite, out upon a landscape farmed by clans of sullen Grays, went the power-wagon. Signs of the Dirdir presence appeared: a gray butte bristling with purple and scarlet towers, overlooking a rift valley, walled by sheer cliffs, which served the Dirdir as a hunting range. On the sixth day a range of mountains rose ahead: the back of the palisades overlooking Hei and Sivishe. The journey was almost at an end. All night the motor-wagon lumbered along a dusty road by the light of the pink and blue moons.

The moons set; the eastern sky took on the color of dried blood. Dawn came as a skyburst of dark scarlet, orange-brown, sepia. Ahead appeared the Ajzan Gulf and the clutter of Sivishe. Two hours later the motor-wagon lumbered into Sivishe Depot beside the bridge.

Chapter 11

Reith and Zap 210 crossed the bridge amid the usual crowd of Grays trudging to and from their work in the Hei factories.

Sivishe was achingly familiar: the background for so much passion and grief that Reith found his heart pounding. If, by fantastic luck, he returned to Earth, could he ever forget those events which had befallen him at Sivishe? "Come," he muttered. "Over here, aboard the transit dray."

The dray creaked and groaned; the dingy districts of Sivishe fell behind; they reached the southernmost stop, where the wagon turned east, toward the Ajzan shore. Ahead lay the salt flats, with a road winding out of Aila Woudiver's construction depot.

All seemed as before: mounds of gravel, sand, slag; stacks of brick and rubble. To the side stood Woudiver's eccentric little office, beyond the warehouse. There was no activity; no moving figures, no drays. The great doors to the warehouse were closed; the walls leaned more noticeably than ever. Reith accelerated his pace; he strode down the road, with Zap 210 walking, then running, then walking.

Reith reached the yard. He looked all around. Desolation. Not a sound, not a step. Silence. The warehouse seemed on the verge of collapse, as if it had been damaged by an explosion. Reith went to the side entrance, looked within. The premises were vacant. The spaceship was gone. The roof had been torn away and hung in shreds. The workshop and supply racks were a shambles.

Reith turned away. He stood looking over the salt flats. What now?

He had no ideas. His mind was empty. He backed slowly away from the warehouse. Over the main entrance someone had scrawled ONMALE. This was the name of the chief-emblem worn by Traz when Reith had first encountered him on the Kotan steppes. The word prodded at Reith's numbed consciousness. Where were Traz and Anacho?

He went to the office and looked within. Here, while he lay sleeping, gas had stupefied him; Gzhindra had tucked him into a sack and carried him away. Someone else now lay on the couch—an old man asleep. Reith knocked on the wall. The old man awoke, opening first one rheumy eye, then the other. Pulling his gray cloak about his shoulders, he heaved himself erect. "Who is there?" he cried out.

Reith discarded the caution he normally would have used. "Where are the men who worked here?"

The door slid ajar; the old man came forth, to look Reith up and down. "Some went here, some went there. One went . . . yonder." He jerked a crooked thumb toward the Glass Box.

"Who was that?"

Again the cautious scrutiny. "Who would you be that doesn't know the news of Sivishe?"

"I'm a traveler," said Reith, trying to hold his voice calm. "What's happened here?"

"You look like a man named Adam Reith," said the caretaker. "At least that's how the description went. But Adam Reith could give me the name of Lokhar and the name of a Thang, that only he would know."

"Zarfo Detwiler is a Lokhar; I once knew Issam the Thang."

The caretaker looked furtively around the landscape. His gaze rested suspiciously on Zap 210. "And who is this?"

"A friend. She knows me for Adam Reith; she can be trusted."

"I have instructions to trust no one, only Adam Reith."

"I am Adam Reith. Tell me what you have to tell me."

"Come here. I will ask a final question." He drew Reith aside and wheezed in his ear: "At Coad Adam Reith met a Yao nobleman."

"His name was Dordolio. Now what is your message?"

"I have no message."

Reith's impatience almost burst through his restraint. "Then why do you ask such questions?"

"Because Adam Reith has a friend who wants to see him. I am to take Adam Reith to this friend, at my own discretion."

"Who is this friend?"

The old man waved his finger. "Tut! I never answer no questions. I obey instructions, no more, and thus I earn my fee."

"Well, then, what are your instructions?"

"I am to conduct Adam Reith to a certain place. Then I am done."

"Very well. Let's go."

"Whenever you are ready."

"Now."

"Come then." The old man started down the road, with Reith and Zap 210 following. The old man halted. "Not her. Just you."

"She must come as well."

"Then we cannot go, and I know nothing."

Reith argued, stormed and coaxed, to no avail. "How far is this place?" he demanded at last.

"Not far."

"A mile? Two miles?"

"Not far. We can be back shortly. Why cavil? The woman will not run away. If she does, find another. So was my style when I was a buck."

Reith searched the landscape: the road, the scattering of huts at the edge of the salt flats, the salt flats themselves. No living creature could be seen: a negative reassurance at best. Reith looked at Zap 210. She looked back with an uncertain smile. A detached part of Reith's brain noted that here, for the first time, Zap 210 had smiled—a tremulous, uncomprehending smile, but nonetheless a true smile. Reith said in a somber voice: "Get in the cabin; bolt the door. Don't open for anyone. I'll be back as soon as I can."

Zap 210 went into the cabin. The door closed; the bolt shot home. Reith said to the old man: "Hurry then. Take me to my friend."

"This way."

The old man hobbled silently along the road, and presently turned aside along a path which led across the salt flats toward the straggle of huts at the edge of Sivishe. Reith began to feel nervous and insecure. He called out: "Where are we going?"

The old man made a vague gesture ahead.

Reith demanded, "Who is the man we are to see?"

"A friend of Adam Reith's."

"Is it . . . Aila Woudiver?"

"I am allowed to name no names. I can tell you nothing."

"Hurry."

The old man hobbled on, toward a hut somewhat apart from the others, an ancient structure of moldering gray bricks. The old man went up to the door, pounded, then stood back.

From within came a stir. Behind the single window was the flicker of movement. The door opened. Ankhe at afram Anacho looked forth. Reith exhaled a great gusty breath. The old man shrilled: "Is this the man?"

Anacho said, "Yes. This is Adam Reith."

"Give me my money then; I am anxious to have done with this line of work."

Anacho went within and returned with a pouch rattling with sequins. "Here is your money. In a month come back. There will be another waiting for you if you have held your tongue meanwhile."

The old man took the pouch and departed.

Reith asked: "Where is Traz? Where is the ship?"

Anacho shook his long pale head. "I don't know."

"What!"

"This is what happened. You were taken by the Gzhindra. Aila Woudiver was wounded but he did not die. Three days after the event the Dirdirmen came for Aila Woudiver, and dragged him off to the Glass Box. He complained, he implored, he screamed, but they took him away. I heard later that he provided a spectacular hunt, running in a frenzy like a bull marmont, braying at the top of his lungs. . . . The Dirdirmen saw the ship when they came to take Aila Woudiver; we feared that they would return. The ship was ready to fly, so we decided to move the ship from Sivishe. I said that I would stay, to wait for you. In the middle of the night Traz and the technicians took the ship up, and flew it to a place that Traz said you would know."

"Where?" Reith demanded.

"I don't know. If I was taken, I wanted no knowledge, so that I could not be forced into betrayal. Traz wrote 'Onmale' on the shed. He said that you would know where to come."

"Let's go back to the warehouse. I left a friend there."

Anacho asked: "Do you know what he means by 'Onmale'?"

"I think so. I can't be sure."

They returned along the trail. Reith asked, "Is the skycar still available for our use?"

"I carry the call-token. I see no reason why there should be difficulty."

"The situation isn't as bad as it might be then. . . . I've had an interesting set of experiences." He told Anacho something of his adventures. "I escaped the Shelters. But along the shore of the Second Sea Gzhindra began to follow. Perhaps they were hired by the Khors; perhaps the Pnume sent them after us. We saw Gzhindra in Urmank; probably these same Gzhindra boarded the *Nhiahar*. They are still on the Saschanese Islands, for all I know. Since then we apparently haven't been followed, and I'd like to leave Sivishe before they pick us up again."

"I'm ready to leave now," said Anacho. "At any instant we may lose our luck."

They turned down the road leading to Woudiver's old warehouse. Reith stopped short. It was as he had feared, in the deepest darkest layer of his subconscious. The door to the office stood ajar. Reith broke into a run, with Anacho coming after.

Zap 210 was nowhere in the office, nor in the ruined warehouse. She was nowhere to be seen.

Directly before the office the ground was damp; the prints of narrow, bare feet were plain. "Gzhindra," said Anacho. "Or Pnumekin. No one else."

Reith gazed across the salt flats, calm in the amber light of afternoon. Impossible to search, impossible to run across salt marsh and flat, looking and calling. What could he do? Unthinkable to do nothing. . . . What of Traz, the spaceship, the return to Earth which now was feasible? The idea sank from his mind like a waterlogged timber, with only the umbral shape, the afterimage, remaining. Reith sat down upon an old crate. Anacho watched a moment, his long white face drawn and melancholy, like that of a sick clown. Finally, in a somewhat hollow voice, he said, "Best that we be on our way."

Reith rubbed his forehead. "I can't go just yet. I've got to think."

"What is there to think about? If the Gzhindra have taken her, she is gone."

"I realize that."

"In such a case, you can do nothing."

Reith looked toward the palisades. "She will be taken back underground. They will swing her out over a dark gulf and after a time drop her."

Anacho hunched his shoulders in a shrug. "You cannot alter this regrettable fact so put it out of your mind. Traz awaits us with the spaceship."

"But I can do something," said Reith. "I can go after her."

"Into the underground places? Insanity! You will never return!"

"I returned before."

"By a freak of fate."

Reith rose to his feet.

Anacho went on desperately: "You will never return. What of Traz? He will wait for you forever. I can't tell him you have sacrificed everything—because I do not know where he is."

"I don't intend to sacrifice everything," said Reith. "I intend to return."

"Indeed!" declared Anacho with a sneer of vast scorn. "This time the Pnume will make sure. You will swing out over the gulf beside the girl."

"No," said Reith. "They will not swing me. They want me for Foreverness."

Anacho threw up his arms in bafflement. "I will never understand you, the most obstinate of men! Go underground! Ignore your faithful friends! Do your worst! When do you go below? Now?"

"Tomorrow," said Reith.

"Tomorrow? Why delay? Why deprive the Pnume of your society a single instant?"

"Because this afternoon I have preparations to make. Come along; let's go into town."

Chapter 12

At dawn Reith went to stand at the edge of the salt flats. Here, months before, he and his friends had detected Aila Woudiver's signals to the Gzhindra. Reith also held a mirror; as Carina 4269 lifted into the sky, he swept the reflection back and forth across the salt flats.

An hour passed. Reith methodically flashed the mirror, apparently to no avail. Then from nowhere, or so it seemed, came a pair of dark figures. They stood half a mile away, looking toward Reith. He flashed the mirror. Step by step they approached, as if fascinated. Reith went to meet them. Gradually the three came together, and at last stood fifty feet apart.

A minute passed. The three appraised each other. The faces of the Gzhindra were shaded under low-crowned black hats; both were pale and somewhat vulpine, with long thin noses and bright black eyes. Presently they came closer. In a quiet voice one spoke: "You are Adam Reith."

"I am Adam Reith."

"Why did you signal us?"

"Yesterday you came to take my companion."

The Gzhindra made no remark.

"This is true, is it not?" Reith demanded.

"It is true."

"Why did you do this?"

"We hold such a commission."

"What did you do with her?"

"We delivered her to such a place as we were bid."

"Where is this place?"

"Yonder."

"You have a commission to take me?"

"Yes."

"Very well," said Reith. "You go first. I will follow."

The Gzhindra consulted in whispers. One said: "This is not feasible. We do not care to walk with others coming at our backs."

"For once you can tolerate the sensation," said Reith. "After all, you will thereby be fulfilling your commission."

"True, if all goes well. But what if you elect to burn us with a weapon?"

"I would have done so before," said Reith. "At the moment I only want to find my companion and bring her back to the surface."

The Gzhindra surveyed him with impersonal curiosity. "Why will you not walk first?"

"I don't know where to go."

"We will direct you."

Reith spoke so harshly that his voice cracked. "Go first. This is easier than carrying me in a sack."

The Gzhindra whispered to each other, moving the corners of their thin mouths without taking their eyes off Reith. Then they turned and walked slowly off across the salt flats.

Reith came after, remaining about fifty feet to the rear. They followed the faintest of trails, which at times disappeared utterly. A mile, two miles, they walked. The warehouse and the office diminished to small rectangular marks; Sivishe was a blurred gray crumble at the northern horizon.

The Gzhindra halted and turned to Reith, who thought to detect a fugitive flicker of glee. "Come closer," said one of the Gzhindra. "You must stand here with us."

Reith gingerly came forward. He brought out the energy gun which he had only just purchased, and displayed it. "This is precautionary. I do not wish to be killed, or drugged. I want to go alive down into the Shelters."

"No fear there, no fear there!" "Have no doubts on that score!" said the Gzhindra, speaking together. "Put away your gun; it is without significance."

Reith held the gun in his hand as he approached the Gzhindra.

"Closer, closer!" they urged. "Stand within the outline of the black soil."

Reith stepped on the patch of soil designated, which at once settled into the ground. The Gzhindra stood quietly, so close now that Reith could see the minute creases in the skin of their faces. If they felt alarm for his weapon they showed none.

The camouflaged elevator descended fifteen feet; the Gzhindra stepped off into a concrete-walled passage. Looking over their shoulders they beckoned. "Hurry." They set off at a swinging trot, cloaks flapping from side to side, Reith came behind. The passage slanted downward; running was without sensible effort. The passage became level, then suddenly ended at a brink; beyond stretched a waterway. The Gzhindra motioned Reith down into a boat and themselves took seats. The boat slid along the surface, guided automatically along the center of the channel.

For half an hour they traveled, Reith looking dourly ahead, the Gzhindra sitting stiff and silent as carved black images.

The channel entered a larger waterway; the boat drifted up to a dock. Reith stepped ashore; the Gzhindra came behind, and Reith ignored their near-transparent glee with as much dignity as he could muster. They signaled him to wait; presently from the shadows a Pnumekin appeared. The Gzhindra muttered a few words into the air, which the Pnumekin seemed to ignore, then they stepped back into their boat and slid away, with pale backward glances. Reith stood alone on the dock with the Pnumekin, who now said: "Come, Adam Reith. We have been awaiting you."

Reith said, "The young woman who was brought down yesterday: where is she?"

"Come."

"Where?"

"The *zuzhma kastchai* wait for you."

A sensation like a draft of cold air prickled the skin of Reith's back. Into his mind crept furtive little misgivings, which he tried to put aside. He had taken all precautions available to him; their effectiveness was yet to be tested.

The Pnumekin beckoned. "Come."

Reith followed, resentful and shamed. They went down a zigzag corridor walled with panes of polished black flint, accompanied by reflections and moving shadows. Reith began to feel dazed. The corridor widened into a hall of black mirrors; Reith now moved in a state of bewilderment. He followed the Pnumekin to a central column, where they slid back a portal. "You must go onward alone, to Foreverness."

Reith looked through a portal, into a small cell lined with a substance like silver fleece. "What is this?"

"You must enter."

"Where is the young woman who was brought here yesterday?"

"Enter through the portal."

Reith spoke in anger and apprehension: "I want to talk to the Pnume. It is important that I do so."

"Step into the cell. When the portal opens, follow, follow the trace, to Foreverness."

In a state of sick fury Reith glared at the Pnumekin. The pale face looked back with fish-like detachment. Demands, threats, rose up in Reith's throat only to dwindle and die. Delay, any loss of time, might result in terrible consequences, the thought of which caused his stomach to jerk and quiver. He stalked into the cell.

The portal closed. Down slid the cell, dropping at a rapid but controlled rate. A minute passed. The cell halted. A portal flew open. Reith stepped forth into black glossy darkness. From his feet a trail of luminous yellow dots wound off into the gloom. Reith looked in all directions. He listened. Nothing, no sound, no pressure of any living presence. Burdened with a sense of destiny, he set off along the trace.

The line of luminous spots swung this way and that. Reith followed them with exactitude, fearing what might lay to either side. On one occasion he thought to hear a far hushed roar, as of air rising from some great depth.

The dark lightened, almost imperceptibly, to a glow from some unseen source. Without warning he came to a brink; he stood at the edge of a darkling landscape, a place of objects faintly outlined in gold or silver luminosity. At his feet a flight of stone steps led down; Reith descended, step after step.

He reached the bottom and halted in an uncontrollable pang of terror; in front of him stood a Pnume.

Reith pulled together the elements of his will. He said in as firm a voice as he could muster: "I am Adam Reith. I have come here for the young woman, my companion, whom you took away yesterday. Bring her here immediately."

From the shape came the husky Pnume whisper: "You are Adam Reith?"

"Yes. Where is the woman?"

"You came here from Earth?"

"What of the woman? Tell me!"

"Why did you come to Old Tschai?"

A roar of desperation rose in Reith's throat. "Answer my question!"

The dark shape slid quietly away. Reith stood a moment, undecided whether to stand or follow.

The gold and silver luminosities seemed to become brighter; or perhaps Reith had begun to cast order upon the seemingly unrelated shapes. He began to see outlines and tracts, pagoda-like frameworks, a range of columns. Beyond appeared silhouettes with gold and silver fringes, as yet unstructured by his mind.

The Pnume stalked slowly away. Reith's frustration reached an intensity where he felt almost faint; then he experienced a rage which sent him bounding after the

Pnume. He seized the harsh shoulder-element and jerked; to his utter astonishment the Pnume dropped as if falling over backward, the arms swinging down to serve as forelegs. It stood ventral surface upmost, head swiveling strangely down and over, so that the Pnume took on the aspect of a night-hound. While Reith gaped in awe and embarrassment the Pnume flipped itself upright, to regard Reith with chilling disfavor.

Reith found his voice. "I must talk to responsible folk among you and quickly. What I have to say is urgent—to you and to me!"

"This is Foreverness," came the husky voice. "Such words have no meaning."

"You will think differently, when you hear me."

"Come to your place in Foreverness. You are awaited." Once more the creature set off. Tears brimmed in Reith's eyes; vast outrage rose up behind his teeth. If anything had happened to Zap 210, they would pay, how they would pay! regardless of consequence.

For a space they walked and presently passed through a columned portal into a new underground realm: a place which Reith associated with some elegant memorial garden of old Earth.

Away and along the gold- and silver-fringed prospect stood brooding shapes. Reith had no opportunity for speculation. Certain shapes moved forward; he saw them to be Pnume, and advanced to meet them. There were at least twenty; by their extreme diffidence and unobtrusiveness Reith understood them to be of the highest status. Facing the twenty shadows in this shadow-haunted corner of Foreverness he could not help but wonder as to the state of his mind. Was he wholly sane? In such surroundings orderly mental processes were inapplicable. By sheer brutal energy he must impose his personal will-to-order upon the devious environment of the Pnume.

He looked around the shadowed group. "I am Adam Reith," he said. "I am an Earthman. What do you want of me?"

"Your presence in Foreverness."

"I'm here," said Reith, "but I intend to go. I came of my own volition; are you aware of this?"

"You would have come in any event."

"Wrong. I would not have come. You kidnapped my friend, a young woman. I came to fetch her away and take her back to the surface."

The Pnume, as if by signal, all took a simultaneous slow step forward: a sinister movement, the stuff of nightmare. "How did you expect to effect so much? This is Foreverness."

Reith thought for a moment. "You Pnume have lived long on Tschai."

"Long, long: we are the soul of Tschai. We are the world itself."

"Other races live on Tschai; they are people more powerful than yourselves."

"They come and go: colored shadows to entertain us. We expel them as we choose."

"You do not fear the Dirdir?"

"They cannot reach us. They know none of our precious secrets."

"What if they did?"

The dark shapes approached another slow pace.

Reith called out in a harsh voice: "What if the Dirdir knew all your secrets: all your tunnels and passages and pop-outs?"

"A grotesque situation which can never be real."

"But it can be real. I can make it real." Reith brought forth a folder bound in blue leather. "Examine this."

The Pnume gingerly accepted the portfolio. "It is the lost master-set!"

"Wrong again," said Reith. "It is a copy."

The Pnume set up a low whimpering sound, and Reith once again thought of the night-hounds; he had often heard just such soft calls out on the Kotan steppes.

The sad half-whispered wails subsided. The Pnume stood in a rigid semicircle. Reith could feel their emotion; it was almost palpable, a crazy, irresponsible ferocity he heretofore had associated only with the Phung.

"Be calm," said Reith. "The danger is not imminent. The charts are hostage to my safety; you are secure unless I do not return to the surface. In this case the charts will be given over to the Blue Chasch and the Dirdir."

"Intolerable. The charts must be secured. There is no alternative."

"This is what I hoped you would say." Reith looked around the half-circle. "You agree to my conditions?"

"We have not heard them."

"I want the woman whom you brought down yesterday. If she is dead, I plan to exact a terrible penalty from you. You will long remember me; you will long curse the name Adam Reith."

The Pnume stood in silence.

"Where is she?" demanded Reith in a rasping voice.

"She is in Foreverness, to be crystallized."

"Is she alive? Or is she dead?"

"She is not yet dead."

"Where is she?"

"Across the Field of Monuments, awaiting preparation."

"You say that she is not yet dead—but is she alive and well?"

"She lives."

"Then you are fortunate."

The Pnume surveyed him with incomprehension, and certain of the group gave near-human shrugs.

Reith said: "Bring her here, or let us go to her, whichever is faster."

"Come."

They set out across the Field of Monuments: statues or simulacra representing folk of a hundred various races. Reith could not avoid pausing to stare in fascination. "Who or what are all these creatures?"

"Episodes in the life of Tschai, which is to say, our own lives. There: the Shivvan who came to Tschai seven million years ago. This is an early crystal, one of the oldest: the memento of a far time. Beyond: the Gjee, who founded eight empires and were expunged by the Fesa, who in turn fled the light of the red star Hsi. Yonder: others who have dropped by along their way to oblivion."

Along the avenues the group moved. The monuments were black, fringed with luminous gold and silver: creatures quadruped, triped, biped; with heads, cerebral bags, nervenets; with eyes, optical bands, flexible sensors, prisms. Here towered a massive bulk with a heavy cranium; it brandished a seven-foot sword. The creature Reith saw to be a Green Chasch bull. Nearby a Blue Chasch chastened a group of crouching Old Chasch, while three Chaschmen glowered from the side. Beyond were Dirdir and Dirdirmen, attended by two men and two women of a race Reith failed to recognize. To the side a single Wankh, alone and austere, surveyed a gang of toiling men. Beyond these groups, except for a single empty pedestal, the avenue led away, down a black slope to a slow black river, the surface marked by drifting silver swirls. Beside the river stood a cage of silver bars; huddled in the cage was Zap 210. She watched the group approach with an impassive face. She saw Reith; her face crumpled into opposed emotions; grief and joy, relief and dismay. She had been stripped of her surface clothes; she wore only a white shift.

Reith took pains to control his voice; still he spoke thickly. "What have you done to her?"

"She has been treated with Liquid One. It invigorates and tones, and opens the passages for Liquid Two."

"Bring her forth."

Zap 210 emerged from the cage. Reith took her hand, stroked her head. "You are safe. We're going back to the surface." He stood for a few minutes quietly waiting while she wept in relief and nervous exhaustion on his shoulders.

The Pnume came close. One said: "The return of all charts is demanded."

Reith managed a thick laugh. "Not yet. I have other demands to make of you—but elsewhere. Let us leave this place. Foreverness oppresses me."

In a hall of polished gray marble Reith faced the Pnume Elders. "I am a man; I am disturbed to see men of my own kind living the unnatural lives of Pnumekin. You must breed no more human children, and the children now underground must be transferred to the surface and there maintained until they are able to fend for themselves."

"But this means the end of the Pnumekin!"

"So it does, and why not? Your race is seven million years old or more. Only in the last twenty or thirty thousand years have you had Pnumekin to serve you. Their loss will be no great hardship."

"If we agree—what of the charts?"

"I will destroy all but a very few copies. None will be delivered to your enemies."

"This is unsatisfactory! We would then live in constant dread!"

"I can't worry as to this. I must retain control over you, to guarantee that my demands have been met. In due course I may return all the charts to you—sometime in the future."

The Pnume muttered disconsolately together a few moments. One said in a flat whisper: "Your demands will be met."

"In this case, conduct us back to the Sivishe salt flats."

At sunset the salt flats were quiet. Carina 4269 hung in a smoky haze behind the palisades, glinting upon the Dirdir towers. Reith and Zap 210 approached the old warehouse. From the office came Anacho's spare form. He stepped forward to meet them. "The sky-car is here. There is nothing to keep us."

"Let's hurry then. I can't believe we're free."

The sky-car lifted from behind the warehouse and swept north. Anacho asked: "Where do we go?"

"To the Kotan steppes, south of where you and I first met."

All night they flew, over the barren center of Kislovan, then over the First Sea and the Kotan marshlands.

At dawn they drifted over the edge of the steppes while Reith studied the landscape below. They crossed a forest; Reith pointed to a clearing. "There: where I came down to Tschai. The Emblem camp lay to the east. There, by that grove of feather-bush: there we buried Onmale. Drop down there."

The sky-car landed. Reith alighted and walked slowly toward the woods. He saw the glint of metal. Traz came forth. He stood quietly as Reith approached. "I knew that you would come."

Traz had changed. He had become a man: something more than a man. On his shoulder he wore a medallion of metal, stone and wood. Reith said: "You dug up the emblem."

"Yes. It called to me. Wherever I walked upon the steppe I heard voices, all the voices of all the Onmale chieftains, calling to be taken up from the dark. I brought forth the emblem; the voices are now silent."

"And the ship?"

"It is ready. Four of the technicians are here. One stayed at Sivishe, two lost heart and set off across the steppes for Hedaijha."

"The sooner we depart the better. When we're actually out in space I'll believe that we've escaped."

"We are ready."

Anacho, Traz and Zap 210 entered the spaceship. Reith took a last look around the sky. He bent, touched the soil of Tschai, crumbled a handful of mold between his fingers. Then he too entered the unlovely hulk. The port was closed and sealed. The generators hummed. The ship lifted toward the sky. The face of Tschai receded; the planet exhibited rotundity, became a gray-brown ball, and presently was gone.

Recommended for Star Warriors!

The Dorsai Novels of Gordon R. Dickson

☐ **DORSAI!** (#UE1432—$1.75)
☐ **SOLDIER, ASK NOT** (#UE1339—$1.75)
☐ **TACTICS OF MISTAKE** (#UW1279—$1.50)
☐ **NECROMANCER** (#UE1481—$1.75)

The Commodore Grimes Novels of A. Bertram Chandler

☐ **THE BIG BLACK MARK** (#UW1355—$1.50)
☐ **THE WAY BACK** (#UW1352—$1.50)
☐ **STAR COURIER** (#UY1292—$1.25)
☐ **TO KEEP THE SHIP** (#UE1385—$1.75)
☐ **THE FAR TRAVELER** (#UW1444—$1.50)

The Dumarest of Terra Novels of E. C. Tubb

☐ **JACK OF SWORDS** (#UY1239—$1.25)
☐ **SPECTRUM OF A FORGOTTEN SUN** (#UY1265—$1.25)
☐ **HAVEN OF DARKNESS** (#UY1299—$1.25)
☐ **PRISON OF NIGHT** (#UW1346—$1.50)
☐ **INCIDENT ON ATH** (#UW1389—$1.50)
☐ **THE QUILLIAN SECTOR** (#UW1426—$1.50)

The Daedalus Novels of Brian M. Stableford

☐ **THE FLORIANS** (#UY1255—$1.25)
☐ **CRITICAL THRESHOLD** (#UY1282—$1.25)
☐ **WILDEBLOOD'S EMPIRE** (#UW1331—$1.50)
☐ **THE CITY OF THE SUN** (#UW1377—$1.50)
☐ **BALANCE OF POWER** (#UE1437—$1.75)

If you wish to order these titles,

please use the coupon in

the back of this book.